Entrance

Opposites Attract Series, Volume 1

Roxie Odell

Published by Dark Shadow Publishing, 2021.

ENTRANCE

First edition. May 1, 2021.

Written by Roxie Odell.

Entrance

A BAD BOY BILLIONAIRE NOVEL

BESTSELLING AUTHOR

ROXIE ODELL

Opposites
ATTRACT
BOOK ONE

Find Roxie Odell:

NEWSLETTER:
http://eepurl.com/bHD6Vr
Facebook Page:
https://www.facebook.com/RoxieOdell

Opposites Attract Series

Book 1 – Entrance
Book 2 – Allure
Book 3 - Enthrall

Entrance Blurb

AT FIRST OPPOSITES attract. Then opposites attack.

Lucas Henry, a billionaire bad boy from the wrong side of the tracks, made his way up from street living to penthouse owner.

A serious lapse in judgment leads him into a huge scandal, so he must do everything he can to repair his reputation with the media and the public. Everything starts going sideways when he wins a date with the fiery small-town veterinarian, Emilia Willow.

Emilia, after dealing with her own sordid past and disastrous relationships, is cautious and careful. She can smell trouble and its name is Lucas.

Lucas' green-energy project was supposed to buy him a ticket right back into the spotlight, not distract him and derail his efforts. Now he has to figure out if Emilia is worth fighting for, even against a meaner-than-hell sheriff, or if he should run back to the rich life.

ROXIE ODELL
ROXIE ODELL
GET IT ON
Google Play
kobo
Available at
amazon
nook
ROXIE
ODELL

Chapter 1

THE AIRPORT WAS PROBABLY the smallest one I had ever seen, with a few runways mostly taken up by small, private prop planes. The concrete runways were cracked and soiled, but they worked okay, or at least, the fact that I was still alive attested to that. I wasn't used to rural areas, but this was all for the project, and it was important that I made the most of it. Driving away from my personal luxury jet was painful, though. I already missed the lush seats, the climate-controlled cabin, and the drinks. I really missed the drinks. The jet had been one of the most exciting purchases of my career, and I decked it out to feel like home, especially since I spent so much time in it. It almost felt strange to see it from the outside, sitting in the barely covered hangar bays.

I wasn't born into the rich life, being the guy from the wrong side of the tracks, or so they called me, but I found that the rich life suited me. I had gotten used to having nearly unlimited money, being able to help whoever I wanted, buy whatever I wanted, and do whatever I wanted without the stress of fiscal limitations. I tried to use my money for positive things, though, things that would help communities, even the world. I felt it was my responsibility to do so, but with that came its own share of critics. Not everyone saw my money and my attempts to help others in a positive light, and that definitely took some getting used to. Until I had made my first million, I'd been pretty naïve at how the world worked.

I stared out the window watching field after field pass by outside. They all looked the same to me except for the occasional spotted cow meandering through the pasture, getting its helping of lush, green grasses. My mind turned to the past and the whirlwind the last decade had been when I literally went from rags to riches in my own life. I had grown up extremely poor, no stranger to the streets. I had hustled since I was old enough to be on my own, trying to help my mother get by. My mother worked two jobs, and though she tried her best to be a good mom, she rarely had time for anything other than work and sleep. My father, well, he was a different story, and one that I tried not to think about.

Before I had boarded my private jet to the West Coast, I had been safely ensconced in my multimillion-dollar lavish penthouse in the building I owned, surrounded by every luxury I could imagine. I had my friends, my technology, my books, and a whole lot of wine, and that was pretty much my life outside the daily grind. It was a dream compared to where I had come from. Now ... well, I was in a place where the cows outnumbered the people three to one, my cell service was spotty at best, and the hope of finding a good bottle of wine had pretty much left my thoughts. It was pretty with the wide-open spaces, the hard-working farmers in the fields, and the feeling of country, but it definitely was anything but home.

We drove for quite a while after leaving the airport, but as the roads became a little less bumpy, the SUV arrived in the small town that would serve as the epicenter for my newest venture. I was excited to see where my ideas would come to fruition, where the people lived that I was trying so hard to get on board with everything, and where I would be spending quite a bit of time for the foreseeable future. My idea had come about one rainy day when I was in the penthouse just reading through the news, thinking about the future of technology, and wondering how I could help with the current environmental crisis. I was billing it as the "Double R Energy Ranch," which was to become a solar farm and experimental compound for green energy.

Bonanza, Oregon, was one of the first places my team had presented to me. It was abundant with sunshine, had plenty of space for innovation, and boasted some of the cheapest real estate in the area. From the stats and the pictures, it was truly the best place to settle down in for the project. This was the first time I had seen it in person and thought it quaint, to say the least. I was starting to see what the team was seeing. When we contacted the city council, they were ecstatic at my interest in placing the ranch there and had sweetened the deal with some pretty lucrative tax breaks. The state itself was more than happy to oblige seeing as they were bending over backward to bring in jobs. It was a win-win for both the company and the community, so it seemed. Still, I hadn't expected everything to be so ... rustic. I was at least expecting maybe a chain fast food joint or a YMCA around the corner or something, but there was nothing. I didn't even realize towns like this still existed, but there I was in the center of it, staring at a whole lot of cows and not many people.

The "downtown" area was not so much of a downtown, more like an area with several buildings built closely together. I counted the blocks and quickly since it was one street less than four blocks long that boasted pretty much all privately owned businesses. I had to admit it was cute, but it made me a little shell-shocked compared to my life in the city where my penthouse was larger than most of the houses dotting the scenery. There wasn't a single traffic light in the whole town, and I was assuming the stop signs were relatively new. I didn't think I had seen a stop sign without graffiti or stickers on it my entire life. The whole place was spotless, not a lick of trash on the ground, and there wasn't a police officer in sight.

As I stared out the SUV window watching the town go by, the driver took a right and pulled up in front of a nondescript brick building looking as if it had been there for at least a hundred years. On the outside, a sign hung above the door, swaying in the breeze. It read, "Rooming House," which I knew was the place I was supposed to be staying while in town. As the SUV parked, I sat there staring at the place, realizing this was the hotel I would be calling home while I was in town. It definitely wasn't the Four Seasons by any stretch of the imagination, but I couldn't imagine many people came to visit the little town of Bonanza very often. At least the front door said there was Wi-Fi, and I would be spending most of my time on-site.

I sighed and climbed out of the car, taking off my gloves and shoving them into my peacoat pockets. The driver grabbed my luggage from the back and headed inside to get me checked in. I smiled at a passing woman with her child and gave a nod, climbing the stairs. I reached down into my pocket and pulled out my phone, looking down at the screen. It was my PR agent, checking in on me as usual. She was more like my babysitter than my PR agent, but I supposed I probably could use her these days.

"Hello," I said.

"Did you get there okay?"

"I did," I said. "I'm walking into the, um, hotel as we speak."

"Good," she said. "Make sure you smile at everyone, hold some conversations, and make yourself look like you fit in."

"I didn't bring my overalls," I whispered.

"Anyway," she said, ignoring my snide comment. "Your new venture is playing out very well in the press. Of course, no one has forgotten about your, well, we'll just call it 'the incident.'"

"Do they ever forget about the bad stuff?"

"Of course not. It sells papers, and you're a gold mine these days, apparently," she said. "Still, I've been working with a few select media outlets, ones that I have good, solid, trustworthy contacts with. I've been arranging tours and interviews for the next couple of weeks. I really hope they'll project a serious image that will replace your current, more negative standing in the media. Something has to give, and we need this project to be a success for you."

"Right," I said, climbing the stairs to the top floor where the company had rented out all the rooms. "Well, I'll do my best to portray that image as well. How much trouble could I get into out here anyway? I'm not much into cow tipping."

"Oh, before I forget because I know you won't remember, the fundraiser is tonight," she said. "I told them you would be in attendance."

"I hate fundraisers," I groaned, walking into my room and nodding at the driver as he set down my luggage and walked back out. "Everyone wants to talk."

"That's kind of the point of it all." She chuckled. "Besides, they may be out in the middle of nowhere, but they still follow the news. Going would be a gesture of goodwill, so you need to look nice, but try not to wear any suits that cost more than most of those people's houses. Put a big smile on your face, and pull out your checkbook. You need to make a sizeable donation."

"I swear it costs more personal funds to start this project than it does to actually pay for the project itself." I sighed. "But it's for a good cause, so I can't really complain."

"You're right," she said. "You can't complain. Call me tomorrow morning, or I'll call you."

"No doubt," I replied, hanging up.

I looked around the room for the first time since I had gotten there and had to admit, I was unenthused by the place I was staying in. It was clean. That was good, but it looked like something from my great-grandmother's house, including the giant box television set. It was about as enthralling as the idea of going to this fundraiser tonight. Thank goodness, it wasn't an auction. The last thing I wanted was to leave with a piece of farm equipment I didn't need just to get the donation up high enough. I wasn't even sure where the fundraiser was, but I was assuming it would be somewhere like a town hall or the gymnasium of the local high school. It definitely would be different from the ballrooms of Manhattan's finest hotels, covered in flowers, chandeliers, and with champagne flowing like rivers.

I turned and walked into the small-tiled bathroom, looking down at the one good thing I had found in the entire place, an old, antique clawfoot tub. It was oversized, which was perfect since I was pretty tall, but had all the charms of an old antique home. It would be the perfect thing to do before getting ready for the fundraiser that night. I put my bags to the side and sighed, turning on the water and undressing. As I sank into the hot, steamy water and laid my head back, I could feel the ease of tension in my shoulders. I wasn't the guy who took baths very often, but after the shock of changing what felt like worlds coming from New York to the little town of Bonanza, I couldn't imagine anything that would have made me more relaxed. Of course, my masseuse definitely would have helped, but that was not an option I had, nor did I think the town offered anything like that. I would make best with what I had and hope it was all worth it in the end.

Chapter 2

Emilia

ALISON HAD BEEN MY best friend for most of my life, and though she was known to get me into some interesting situations, this one topped the list. I didn't even know how it happened. One minute, everything was going fine, and the next minute, I was standing behind the stage feeling more nervous than I had in a really long time, including the time I puked during a fifth-grade chorus concert. I looked up at the grand ceilings of Grange Hall, watching the lights move and shift above. There were people on the catwalk of the stage, making sure everything was perfect. I, on the other hand, was standing backstage, wearing my decade-old prom dress, which was considerably tighter ten years later. It was the fanciest thing I had in my closet, and the last thing I was going to do was go shopping for a dress right before the event. I hated dresses, but I hated shopping even more, so I cinched up my waist and squeezed into the long, tight blue dress, hoping I didn't pass out.

Alison had been coined the planner for the event, and in her mind, she saw everything grand and sparkling. She seemed to forget we were in Grange Hall in Bonanza, Oregon, not some elegant hotel in New York City. She did her best, though, and I had to admit, she'd decorated it well for an event with a very low budget. She had insisted the event be formal and that we all wear floor-length gowns. I couldn't tell if that request was to keep some of the town's debutantes from wearing dresses shorter than appropriate or just because she liked the glitter of it all.

It was the annual fundraiser for the Dream of Wind horse rescue. Dream of Wind was a sanctuary for injured or discarded horses, and it had been my best friend's dream since she was a child. I could remember when we were kids sitting around her mother's stables talking about the future. I was going to be a vet, and that's what I became, but Alison had wanted to save the world. Luckily, she battened down those dreams a bit and focused on horses. I completely supported her dream from the beginning and made sure I got a degree that included large-breed animals like horses so I could help. I loved animals, no matter what they were, and Alison and I worked really well together. I volunteered almost all my free time to helping care for the animals. I went over in the mornings to administer medications, checked on them after work, and went over on the weekends to help her give physical therapy to the ones that needed it. My life was pretty much nothing but furry friends, but I was okay with that.

Every year, Alison worked, planned, and barely slept just to make the fundraiser worth it. It was the bread and butter of the organization, and the money made from this one fundraiser pretty much fed all the horses for the entire year and helped maintain at least half of their medication. The rest of the funds came from other small events, sponsors, and me, of course, a sucker for an animal in need. She threw an enormous fundraiser, with everyone from town filing into Grange Hall for the event. Well, at least, it was huge if filling Grange Hall counted. By Bonanza standards, though, it was definitely a hot ticket. People waited all year to come to the event and see what craziness Alison had planned. They also liked to see the good things Bonanza was doing. The people of the town were all really down-home people. Most of them had hearts of gold and really viewed the world through Bonanza's eyes. Alison's project had been a hit since the first day and gave people a place to take their horses so they wouldn't have to put them down.

I worked every year right beside Alison, trying to get her fundraiser up and running. We had planned an auction of sorts for this year where we would auction off dates with the town's most eligible girls. Everyone was excited about it, and I'd spent weeks going around getting the perfect women to participate. However, as the event grew closer and then the day arrived, I found myself on the hook for more than making arrangements. I was one of the women to be auctioned off, and I was not happy about it in the least. Turned out, Miss Klamath County had a chemistry final the next day and couldn't even make it to the event, much less the auction. I knew school was important, but I had a sneaking suspicion it had something to do with her boyfriend and the fact that she didn't want to end up on a date with some old farmer from down the road. When Alison had mentioned me, I had called that girl right up and begged her, telling her I would even call her professor and get a pass on the exam for a couple of days for her. She was resolute, though, so there I stood.

Alison and I had argued about it for hours, and I told her I would find her a suitable replacement, but she wasn't having it. She said Miss Klamath County had been the biggest draw to the event that year, and whoever was going to replace her had to be equally as awesome. I thought she was talking about someone else until she handed me the pin and told me to ditch the boots and replace them with a pair of heels for the night. I just about died. I had a pretty high self-esteem, and I was glad my best friend had such a high estimation of my appeal to the gentlemen in the crowd, but I thought she might be overhyping me just a bit. Almost everyone in town knew me as the girl constantly covered in something, whether it be dog hair or mud or worse. I doubted anyone in the crowd was chomping at the bit to go on a date with the one who'd neutered old Spot last winter or delivered the farm's cows. Either way, I was there, and I was more than nervous.

I was a small-town girl who grew up in a big, old farmhouse smack dab in the middle of a dairy farm. I went to a local college, got my degree, and moved back to Bonanza where I was the only veterinarian within a fifty-mile radius. I was an animal lover, not the belle of the ball, but Alison thought differently, and I didn't know if that was her yearning for the fundraiser to go well or her clouded view of how desirable her best friend really was. I did know one thing, though. If I didn't fall down at some point because of the heels, it would be a miracle.

I peeked out through the curtains and shuttered at the crowd gathered outside. Everyone in town was there, decked out in their best clothes. Even old, plain Mrs. Weatherby, the local grocer's wife had dolled herself up. This was going to be an interesting evening. Just then, I looked down as Alison's hands slid around my waist, and she squeezed me tightly. I groaned, feeling what little air was in my lungs quickly extinguish.

"You look beautiful," she whispered. "Seriously, you haven't looked this girlie since, well, ever actually. Didn't you wear rain boots with this dress at prom?"

"It was raining," I said in my defense. "And my date had decided dinner on the farm was going to be romantic. I looked like a drowned rat by the time I got to prom. The only thing still dry on me were my feet."

"Well, you look beautiful now, and that's all that matters," she said.

"This is only slightly true if I can somehow figure out how to keep my gut sucked in all night long." I laughed. "Then, I have to worry about whether my brain has enough oxygen getting to it."

"Glamourous people can't afford to breathe comfortably," she said, laughing. "I don't think I've breathed comfortably in public since we were kids and naturally had no gut."

Just hearing the sound of our laughter calmed my nerves. Alison had always had that effect on me, lightening the mood when I thought I would completely fall apart. I knew I was taking the whole thing too seriously, but Alison wasn't the one to have to go on a date with a random guy after the fundraiser was over. Alison's on and off again boyfriend, Jimmy, made sure she didn't become one of the girls being auctioned, and Alison knew he'd spend his entire savings account to keep another guy away from her.

I stepped to the side as the other girls talked loudly and began to line up backstage. They were all girly girls, either pageant contestants or local girls Alison knew would bring in the money. I was the only one there with a down and dirty job, and that was going to be interesting to watch. Alison walked up beside me with her notes in her hand.

"So, Jimmy forgot the one thing I asked him not to forget when we were bringing everything over to the hall today," she said, rolling her eyes. "The damn twinkle lights, which you know are one of the most important parts of the decorations."

"Oh, no," I fake-gasped. "Not the twinkle lights."

"Yep," she said, shaking her head. "I told him to walk his ass back over to the house and get them back to the hall ASAP. On his way back, they came undone, and he showed up with them wrapped around himself, trying to keep them from dragging. I coaxed him over to the wall and plugged them in, letting him stand there twinkling in front of everyone."

"You guys are ridiculous." I laughed. "Like two old married people."

"Don't curse me like that," she whispered with a smile. "All right. It's showtime, girl."

"Please, take it easy on me," I begged. "Just get me on and off that stage as fast as possible, and ignore any bids from my ex."

"I got you on the ex-part," she smiled with a wink.

"Alison," I said with an authoritative tone.

She ignored me and waved, walking off onto the stage. I could hear everyone in the audience begin to quiet as Alison approached the microphone. All the girls in line were whispering and giggling excitedly, and then there was me, clawing at my dress and letting out a deep sigh. I knew it was too much to ask her to go easy on me. She was enjoying my suffering and pain way too much to quit at that point. I would just have to suck it up and smile, knowing the night's auction would really help out the horses back at the stables.

"First, I want to thank everyone for coming out to our annual fundraiser benefiting my nonprofit organization, Dream of Wind," she said into the mic. "Also, I would like to thank the town council for donating Grange Hall for the event."

She paused, letting everyone clap and cheer loudly. When the crowd had calmed, she cleared her throat. It was time for the rules.

"The auction tonight will be for one evening of dinner for the highest bidder with the girl they bid on," she said. "Let's remind everyone of what happened last year with the black eye, so boys, be polite to your dates, and everyone remember, the money goes to an amazing cause. Let's first start with Bridgett Alloy from right here in Bonanza."

Alison went through girl after girl, saving me for last. She had completely ignored my request, but it didn't surprise me in the least. Finally, after everyone else had gone, I heard my name called. I took in a deep breath and walked out under the lights, a complete bundle of nerves.

Chapter 3

Lucas

"SO NICE TO MEET YOU," I said, plastering a smile on my face as I met each of the town elders.

They were all very nice, though I was afraid that as old as they were, I might break something shaking each of their hands. Grange Hall was small and smelled like musty wood, kind of like my grandfather's basement in New York. I had to admit, though, it was fairly tastefully decorated ... if you squinted when looking at the Christmas lights decorating every available surface, and they twinkled too. How nice. I was on my third whiskey, and I needed to remember to thank the organizers for including a bar along with the cheap spaghetti dinner and salad bar that I paid for but passed on.

The first round of the auction was fairly simple, and I had bid a thousand dollars for an overnight at a local winery bed-and-breakfast, figuring if I didn't use it while I was there, I would give it as a gift to one of the councilmen and his wife. The bid was well above the hundred-dollar previous bid, and I was satisfied with my purchase. I figured it would be enough to build some goodwill with the town and help out a cause that was actually pretty neat for a small town like this. If nothing else, my PR rep would get off my tail for at least a few hours, and I might get to drink some wine later on in the week. I looked down at the time and then around the room, making sure I had said hello to all the important people. I figured it was about time I hit the road and headed back to my hotel for the night. I was pretty sure I saw a liquor store on the way over and could make sure to stock up on some whiskey for the hotel room. I had a feeling I was going to need it while I was there.

As I turned, the owner of the organization took the stage again, announcing the next round of auctions. I laughed to myself, realizing it was going to be a girl auction. I tried to hide a smirk as all the guys shimmied up to the front, and the women stood in the back gossiping to each other. Why did every fundraiser run by a woman include the same old song and dance? It was like it was written into code that if you had a fundraiser and you were a woman, you had to auction each other off like cattle. You bid whatever you wanted and tried for a date with one of the town's most eligible women. The women seemed to be as excited as the men about the whole thing, and I had a feeling this was a really big deal in Bonanza, though from the comment about the black eye, last year didn't sound too successful. Maybe it was some weird rite of passage for a woman, or maybe it was just a really good way of drawing money from the men's tight pockets.

I turned and stuck my hands in my pockets, unable to look away. It was like a train wreck, and I had to see who was going to come out on that stage. I mean, what kind of women could really be left eligible in a Podunk town like Bonanza? Most of the women grew up looking for a husband so they could raise some children and eventually become one of the snickering old women in the back. As the girls started walking out on the stage and interviewed with the perky emcee, I found myself actually surprised at how well put together and hot they all were. There was no one I was interested in bidding on, but they were definitely more interesting than the New York City socialites I was used to seeing at functions like this. They had spunk to them, and I could tell almost every single one of them had a twinkle in their eye, looking for the next husband in line. It was both amusing and incredibly interesting to watch.

When it was down to the last girl, I was about to leave, but then Emilia Willow walked out on the stage, and I couldn't budge my feet. She was wearing a skintight blue gown with sequins that sparkled in the Christmas lights. Her dark, shimmering hair had fiery highlights and gave her a dangerous edge. I cleared my throat and turned back, feeling an instantaneous feeling of want in the pit of my stomach. There was something about this girl that hit me like a ton of bricks. I had to stop myself from bidding, remembering that I was only going to be there for a couple of weeks, weeks when I needed to stay focused and on my game. These couple of weeks were just enough time to do what I came to Bonanza to do. I needed to get my ranch going, get everything set up and working correctly, and then give some interviews to the reporters that the PR company had sent out. Those, I needed to be on my game for, knowing I needed good press to polish my public image.

Small town Emilia did not look like the kind of girl who was up there to fool around. She also didn't look like the girl looking for a husband like the rest of them. I could tell there was a fire to her, something she might be trying to hide behind that pretty blue dress and heels, but something I could see right through. It almost made me want her that much more.

"Our last contestant is Emilia Willow," the emcee said. "For those of you who don't know Emilia, she was born and bred right here in Bonanza. She's a veterinarian, also able to make house calls for those who need it, just an FYI. And in her spare time, Emilia donates her skills to the organization, working tirelessly with the horses."

A hometown, house-calling, veterinarian who had a knack for volunteering her time. I definitely needed to stay away from this girl. I needed to stay far, far away from her, in fact, and no matter how much I was yearning to take her out, I needed to remember what I was in that town to do in the first place. Too bad I didn't have any pets, though. That would be one house call I would love to have had. Emilia's look and background screamed that she was a "good girl" from her head to her toes, and me? Well, I was a bad boy and had been for most of my adult life. It wasn't on purpose, but I was never the one to be tied down and had this uncanny knack for accidentally hurting almost every girl I took out. That was more than evident by the trail of broken hearts that followed me everywhere I seemed to go. It was the reason I was in a mess or dramatic situation almost all the time, and it was more than a little annoying and distracting when I thought about it.

I figured I would stand there and watch, having never actually seen one of those auctions take place before then. I had a feeling Emilia was going to be a town favorite, and even the old, catty women in the back were smiling and waving at her. She was the town sweetheart. I had every intention of not bidding, but when it started, I changed my mind really fast. I watched the crowd hearing different bids being shouted out. They started innocently enough with twenty-five dollars here, thirty dollars there, and so on. Then, out of nowhere, a deep voice bellowed out.

"One hundred dollars," the voice shouted.

I followed the voice over to the side where a tall, thick man in a cowboy hat was standing. He had a gold star tacked to his old school leather jacket and his face was firm. Everyone got silent in the crowd, and no one else bid any further. It was like they were afraid of the guy or something. I had a sneaking suspicion it had nothing to do with the dollar amount and more about the size and stature of the man. He was obviously someone important in town, but it was crazy to me how everyone cowered back. I looked back on the stage at Emilia whose face had tightened, and the emcee cleared her throat uncomfortably. There was a sudden flash of fear in her eyes as she looked over at the woman with the mic, obviously trying to signal her without making a scene.

I didn't know what it was, whether it was the look of fear on Emilia's face or the hush of the crowd around me, but something happened inside of me. Suddenly, there was no way I could let this girl walk off that stage with that man. I took in a deep breath and then raised my hand nonchalantly.

"Two hundred dollars," I said loudly from the back.

Everyone immediately turned their heads toward me, including who I now realized was the sheriff. He frowned at me across the room, trying to bully me into submission. I had seen worse, especially growing up on the streets, so some wannabe cowboy wasn't going to shake me.

"Three hundred," the sheriff said, staring me in the face.

I smiled and nodded my head at him, thinking quickly. There was no way this guy was going to bully me. I shuffled in my stance for a moment and then looked up at the emcee.

"Four hundred," I said with a grin.

Everyone's heads were moving back and forth between us as we bid higher and higher. He bid five hundred, I bid seven hundred, and then finally, he smirked and bid one thousand dollars. Obviously, this guy didn't know who he was dealing with.

"Wow," I said with a smile. "That's impressive. I bid five thousand dollars."

Everyone in the room gasped and looked back to the sheriff whose mouth fell open for a second. I couldn't help but chuckle at his reaction. I looked up at the girls on the stage, and the emcee collected herself quickly.

"Sold to the highest bidder for five thousand dollars," she shouted excitedly.

Everyone started to clap loudly, cheering in my direction. I was pretty sure I had just become the new hero of the town. My eyes shot back over to the sheriff who was now throwing daggers at me with his eyes. He turned and disappeared out the door, followed by a squirrely-looking chubby man in a smaller cowboy hat. I looked up at Emilia who looked relieved, nodding at me and then disappearing offstage. I downed the rest of my whiskey and wandered over to the table to pay for my purchases. Everyone stared quietly at me as I walked along, whispering to each other. I nodded at the mayor who tipped his hat at me and smiled uncomfortably. Obviously, what I had just done ruffled more than a few feathers, and I hoped I hadn't gotten into the middle of something I was going to regret. She'd looked like a damsel in distress, and I was definitely a sucker for a girl in need, though in my gut,

I had a feeling she could take care of herself just fine. I guessed I would soon find out.

Chapter 4

Emilia

I PUSHED MY WAY THROUGH the backstage area, not even bothering to grab my coat or say anything to Alison. I pushed through the back door of Grange Hall and started for the parking lot. I had known it would be a mistake participating in the auction, but Alison had ambushed me at the last minute. How was I supposed to tell my best friend no, especially when it benefitted the animals I loved so much? I had accepted and tried to put on a brave face for it, but still, somewhere in the back of mind, I knew something like that was going to happen. I kept asking myself, "What if Janson bids on you?" I didn't actually think he would, though, and I didn't think it would go as far as it did. I had done everything I could to ignore that voice, from trying to be girly and beautiful, to convincing myself Janson wasn't that stupid. Apparently, I was the stupid one, though, because my fears had been realized as he stood there in a showdown with a perfect stranger.

I stopped halfway across the parking lot and bent over, putting my hands on my knees and breathing heavily. I had almost been bought by my ex, someone I had vowed I would never speak to again. I knew it gave him some sick pleasure knowing he could buy me, thinking, as always, that he could get away with anything he wanted since he was the sheriff in town. But he had lost, and that was what was most important. He had not won a date with me, and I could go back to living my life. I stood up and started toward the car again, trying to calm myself down. Some stranger, someone I had never seen in town before who stuck out like a sore thumb in the back of the room, had just paid five thousand dollars to take me out on the town. I wish I had gotten a better look at him before leaving, but the lights on the stage blinded me, making the man more of a shadow than anything else. He wanted to pay all that money to take me on a date, for me to show him the town, not that there was much of a "town" to speak of. We were one of the smallest places left in the United States.

I shook my head and reached down into my purse, trying to find the keys to my truck. I searched through the bag until I found them, groaning as I reached for the door. Before I could, though, a hand grabbed my arm and yanked me back. I dropped my purse on the ground and gasped, knowing that feeling all too well. Slowly, I turned around and that fear from inside came tumbling back to me so fast, it made my head spin. My eyes moved up that old, leather jacket and over the shimmering sheriff's badge, finding Janson staring down at me. He looked angry, angrier than I had seen him in a while. I straightened myself up and looked down at his hand still holding my arm.

"Please, let go of me," I said with a brave face.

He smirked and tightened his grip even harder on my arm. I pulled my arm, but he was too strong. When I looked back up at him, I could see someone standing in the background keeping watch. It was his goon, Gary, lurking not far behind, as always. He had his sidekick wherever he went, and it had become a normal sight for people to see out in town.

"I come out here to support the only organization in this town, and what do I find? You're selling yourself to a crowd of hungry men like you're nothing more than cheap trash," he growled.

"What are you doing bidding then?" I said, feeling the sting of his words. "If you think I'm nothin' but cheap trash, why would you waste your money?"

He tightened his jaw, and the spot under his right eye began to twitch. My stomach dropped, and alarms started going off in my head. That was not a good sign, a sign that I had seen more than once in my lifetime and would really not like to experience again. Janson had always been quick to anger, even when he was younger. I could tell by the grip of his hand and how he was looking at me that he was inches away from completely exploding, and I didn't want to be anywhere near him when he did. It was never a good thing. Immediately, my mind flashed back to one of our last arguments before we had completely split up. I had caught him cheating on me with a waitress from the saloon across town. He never did like being questioned, and never found fault in anything he did. It was infuriating but dangerous as well. It always set him off when I spoke against him.

We had dated for a long time, and in that time, there had been more than one instance where I'd accused him of cheating. Up until that time, though, I'd never had proof, but with the text messages I'd found on his phone, I knew I'd finally had caught him in a lie. Immediately, he had started berating me, reminding me that if I wasn't so unattractive, if I had taken more time to do my hair, my makeup, and not always be working, he wouldn't have to step out on me with other women. He always blamed me for anything he did wrong. I didn't hold back that night, though. I'd had enough of being treated like that. He had humiliated me in front of everyone in the town and broken my heart just the same. I told him to get out, that I didn't want to speak to him anymore, but he refused, telling me he was the one who gave the orders.

When you were in a relationship like that for so long, you started to get tired of being treated that way. That night, I'd had enough, and I lost it, screaming at him to get out of my house before slapping him right across the face. As soon as my hand hit his skin, I knew I shouldn't have done it, but what was done was done, and I stood tall behind my choice. I remembered the muscle under his eye twitching right before he grabbed me by the hair and dragged me through the house into the bedroom. He threw me down on the bed and stared at me, angrier than hell. He pulled his body over mine, holding my arms above my head and jamming his leg between my thighs. I was terrified, more terrified than I had ever been in my life of what was going to come next. I didn't put anything past that man.

My fear had gotten the best of me, and I'd started to cry, begging him to stop. All he did was look down at me and snort in disgust before letting go. He pulled himself to his feet and walked right out of the house, slamming the door behind him. I had just laid there, sobbing into the covers, feeling the burn on my wrists and the pounding in my head. Right then, in the empty back parking lot of Grange Hall, I could see that same dangerous light in his eyes. It put a fear in my throat that forced me to swallow hard and release the tension from under his hand. As much as I wanted to tell him off, I knew that buttoning up my lip might be the wiser way to go. I didn't need a complete scene out there in the parking lot, and I was scared of what he might do to me. I gathered myself and took a deep breath, letting it out slowly.

"Alison asked me to be in the auction at the last second," I said. "The beauty queen that was supposed to be there had canceled, and I had to fill in for her. I didn't want to do it, but you know how important this whole thing is. I couldn't tell her no, not after all the work she had put in."

He snickered, eyeing me up and down, focusing in on the tightness of the dress in my mid-region. I pulled one arm across me, feeling uncomfortable and exposed. He was such an asshole.

"Trust me." He chuckled. "No one would confuse you with a beauty queen."

"Let me go," I said angrily, yanking my arm away from him again.

He snarled, gripping me even tighter, pulling me toward him. His hand was so tight around my arm that it was painful, and I knew it was going to leave a mark. I wasn't going to give into him, though. I couldn't be afraid of him forever.

"Didn't you hear her, pal?" a voice said from behind me. "Let her go."

I turned toward the shadowy figure, recognizing him immediately as the man who had bought me during the auction. Both relief and fear ran through my chest, knowing I wasn't alone but that Janson wasn't going to let go so easily. I tried to pull away, but he had his hand so tight, I could barely move.

"Move on," Janson growled. "This is none of your damn business."

The man wasn't scared off that easily, though, and I could hear his shoes tapping across the pavement as he moved closer. I turned my head toward him, and as he stepped forward into the street lights, my heart fluttered in my chest. He was the most handsome man I had ever seen, in Bonanza or anywhere else. I had to admit, it took me by complete surprise. Janson kept his hand tightly gripped on my arm, not giving in to the man's advances.

"Let her go," he said sternly. "You lost fair and square, and that isn't her fault. If you want to take it up with someone, why don't you take it up with me? Or do you like an unfair fight with a girl in a dark parking lot?"

I looked between the two of them, feeling uncomfortable being stuck in the middle. The two of them stared each other down, no words being spoken between them. I held my breath, terrified of what was going to happen next. It felt like the two of them were standing there staring at each other for hours. Janson looked the man up and down before releasing my arm, tossing me back. The man grabbed my shoulders and kept me on my feet, letting go as I stood up and rubbed my arm. Janson looked back at me and snorted, turning and stalking off. He whistled and tossed his hand, his sidekick, Gary, following quickly behind him like a whipped puppy.

I had never seen Janson back down from a fight, and I didn't know if it was the fact that we were standing in a parking lot in the middle of town or that he was intimidated by the man standing beside me. Either way, I was glad he was gone, and I could let out a deep breath. I stood there, rubbing my arm, feeling like I needed to say something.

This was the second time in one night this man had saved me from Janson's clutches, and I had never met him before in my life. How much more insane could my life really get before something started to give?

Chapter 5

Lucas

MY BLOOD WAS RACING, and I hadn't found myself this upset in a really long time. I could feel the anger boiling up inside of me, and I didn't even know how I had gotten to that point, standing in that parking lot, staring at this idiot with his hands on a woman like that. After I'd checked in at the payment desk, they told me to go find Alison, the emcee and owner of the organization. I had tracked her down with a check in hand, finding her backstage finishing up a few things.

"Thank you so much," she said, shaking my hand. "I'm Alison."

"Lucas." I smiled. "Just figured I would touch base with my date. Do you know where I could find her?"

"Hmm, that's a good question," she said. "Seriously, though, your bid will do so much for our horses. Just your bid on Emilia alone will pay for a lot of the medication needed to keep these horses alive and comfortable. It's been a long time since anyone has put that kind of money into our organization, and that's on top of the bed and breakfast they said you won the bid on. It's very generous. I'm just glad you were able to win the bid with Emilia."

I smiled, watching the relief on Alison's face. Between the look on her face and the relief that I had seen on Emilia's before she disappeared off stage, I couldn't help wondering what was going on. There was obviously something up with the guy who'd been bidding, something that made everyone silent and made the two girls nervous as hell.

"So, I'm curious," I said with a charming smile. "Who was that guy bidding against me? The one with the leather and the badge. I'm assuming he's some kind of officer in town, maybe the sheriff. I just couldn't help but notice how everyone reacted to him."

The smile moved off Alison's face, and her eyes clouded over. She looked past me at the curtain, obviously thinking but not saying a word. She shook her head and smiled again, pulling herself out of it.

"Why don't we go look for Emilia?" she said, taking me by the arm and walking me out on the stage.

We looked throughout the entire room, but there was no sign of her anywhere. She was hard to miss in that dress with that beautiful smile, but it looked like she was already gone. Alison turned to me and shook her head.

"She must have had to leave," she said. "Let me take down your number."

"Alison," one of the girls called from backstage. "I need you for a second."

"Give me one minute." She smiled.

Instead of waiting, I figured I would take a chance and run out to the parking lot. Maybe I could catch Emilia before she left for the night. I went out the front door and walked around the building to the back parking lot. The street lights were few and far between, but as I turned the corner, I'd seen her standing there with the sheriff, his hand clutching her arm, and her purse on the ground. Immediately, I was irritated, and I started walking toward them. Generally, I was a calm, collected person, relatively cold in my business dealings. I had never been the guy who let much get to me, but as I walked forward, looking at the situation, I could feel the anger start to build up inside of me rapidly.

"Let me go," Emilia demanded to the guy.

I stood there looking at them, waiting to see what he was going to do. From the twitch under the sheriff's eye and the look on his face, it didn't seem he was the kind of man who took orders from anyone, much less a woman. I could see him grasping her arm tighter, and that was the moment I decided to step in.

"Didn't you hear her, pal?" I said, standing in the shadow of the light. "Let her go."

"Move on," the sheriff growled. "This is none of your damn business."

He gripped onto Emilia tighter, staring over in my direction. Slowly, I walked forward into the light, looking at Emilia and then back up at him. It was obvious this guy wasn't going to let go, not anytime soon. He wasn't happy I was interfering, but I didn't back down from anyone.

"Let her go," I said sternly. "You lost fair and square, and that isn't her fault. If you want to take it up with someone, why don't you take it up with me? Or do you like an unfair fight with a girl in a dark parking lot?"

I was seconds away from saying "fuck it" and paying for the inevitable lawsuit that would follow after beating the shit out of the guy, but he finally stepped down, tossing Emilia at me and walking away. I grabbed her by the shoulders and steadied her, watching as he whistled out to his sidekick. Emilia reached up and rubbed her arm, watching until the sheriff was nowhere in sight.

"Thanks," she mumbled, looking like she was seconds away from tears. "He can really be an asshole sometimes. Thank you, really. I'm not really sure what he would have done if you hadn't walked up. He was angrier than I've seen him in a long time."

"Who is he?"

"The sheriff." She sighed. "His name is Janson."

"Did he hurt you?" I asked her.

I could feel my rage climbing another notch at the thought of her being manhandled by the sheriff or anyone else for that matter. I didn't know where the anger was coming from, but I still felt like I could beat the shit out of the guy. He sure seemed to deserve a good ass kicking.

"No," she said quietly, shaking her head and looking at the ground. "Nothing that won't go away in a couple of days."

Just the thought of a bruise on her arm made me feel terrible for not doing more. I had never been one to think any violence toward a woman was ever warranted, but with her, it was like this crazy want to take away the pain and fear I knew she was feeling. I had never felt that protective of anyone before in my life, and I wondered why it was surfacing there in that moment. Maybe it was because I saw it happening, or maybe it was her, the girl from the stage, the one I had paid five thousand dollars to go on a date with. She pulled her other arm over her chest and rubbed both shoulders, shivering in the cold night air. I pulled my jacket off and slowly moved toward her, draping it over her shoulders. She pulled it around her, and I backed away, trying not to make her feel uncomfortable at all. I knew I was a stranger, and I knew I had walked up on a private moment that she might be feeling all kinds of emotions about.

"Thank you," she said, looking up at me.

Her eyes looked almost golden in the moonlight, and I was completely struck by how absolutely beautiful she was. Sure, I had been frozen in place when I'd seen her on stage, but up close, she was even more stunning than I had originally thought. I could barely take my eyes off her. I felt drawn to her in that moment like we were the only two people in the entire world. Her eyes were mesmerizing, and before I even knew what I was doing, I pulled my hands up and cupped her face, stroking her cheeks with my thumbs. We stood there like that for several moments, unable to pull away, not wanting to pull away from each other. It was like a trance I had never experienced before in my life. Without thinking, I opened my mouth and began to talk.

"A woman as beautiful as you should be treasured," I said, shaking my head. "Not insulted. I don't care what happened between the two of you, that man had no right to touch you like that. You deserve so much more."

I could feel a rush of electricity move from my hands, down my arms, and into my chest. My heart began to beat faster and faster, and my breath was caught in my throat. All of it was from the feeling of her skin touching mine. Her eyes widened, and she whimpered slightly at my words. From her reaction, I was pretty sure she was feeling the same thing I was. I swallowed hard and pulled my hands down, putting them in my pockets. I chuckled and looked around at her truck. She leaned down and picked up her purse, grabbing the different pieces off the ground and shoving them in. I leaned down and picked up her keys, looking forward into her eyes. We both paused again as I handed her the keys and stood up.

"Why don't you let me drive you home?" I said, noticing how shaken she looked.

"That's okay." She smiled. "I don't live very far and wouldn't have even driven if it weren't for the outfit and the all the stuff I had to bring over. I'm sure I'll be fine. I can make it back on my own."

"I'm more than sure you can make it home," I said. "You look like you're a very tough girl, but tonight, you don't have to. Think about it as me wooing you into a date."

"You mean the date you already paid for?" She laughed.

"Yes, that one." I smiled. "Just because I bought it, doesn't mean you don't deserve to be taken care of beforehand."

I reached my hand out for her keys and smiled at her, feeling the butterflies in my chest going wild. She stood there for a moment, staring at me with my jacket still over her shoulders. I knew she was trying to decide whether or not to let me drive her, but from the look in her eyes, I could tell that she wanted to.

"Come on, I promise to be a gentleman." I chuckled.

"All right." She smirked. "Only because you asked nicely."

I walked around to the passenger side of the truck and helped her inside, smiling as I shut the door. I climbed into the passenger seat and started to pull out of the parking lot. She was quiet as we drove, except for giving directions of where to turn.

"At the next stop sign, take a right," she said sweetly.

I glanced over at her sitting in the chair next to me. I still couldn't get over how gorgeous she was. Her tight blue dress hugged every wonderful curve in her body, and her breasts were firm and round. She was probably one of the most beautiful women I had ever seen, and oddly enough, she was tucked away in some small town in Oregon.

"Second house on your right," she said. "The one with the red door."

"Perfect," I replied.

I pulled up in the driveway and stopped at the top, putting the car in drive and turning off the ignition. I handed her the keys and smiled. She blushed, taking them from me and putting them into her purse. She paused and looked over at me.

"If you drove me here, how are you going to get back to your house or hotel?"

"Is it that obvious I'm not from here?" I laughed.

"This town has five hundred people in it." She smirked. "It's kind of obvious. There aren't any taxis in Bonanza."

"Not a problem," I said, pulling out my phone.

I looked at the number on her house and texted my driver, sending the message and waiting a moment. I could feel her looking at me, but I stared down at my phone until a reply came through. I smiled, and put my phone back in my pocket.

"All is solved," I said. "My driver will be here in ten minutes. You don't mind hanging out with me for ten minutes, do you?"

All she did was smile.

Chapter 6

Emilia

I SMILED AT HIM AND got out of the car, walking around and standing in front of it. He followed me, leaning up against the hood and looking up at the stars. I tried to focus and not get caught up in this gorgeous guy in front of me, but it was difficult.

"I don't think I've ever seen this many stars," he said.

While he was staring up at the sky, I was staring at him, watching his profile in the starlight. I could feel my breathing intensify, and I tried to focus back up at the sky. However, I found myself looking back at him out of the corner of my eye. He was stunningly attractive with all the perfect features, the blond wavy hair, and the tight muscles. On top of all of that, he seemed to be a really nice guy. There definitely had to be something wrong with him. My first clue was the fact that he was in Bonanza, and he didn't live there. What the hell was a guy like that doing all the way out here in the middle of nowhere anyway?

"You never told me your name," I said.

"Oh, how rude of me." He chuckled. "I'm Lucas."

"Nice to meet you," I smiled. "So, what the hell are you doing all the way out here in Bonanza. I mean, we've already established you aren't from here."

"That's a good question," he said, flashing me his charming smile. "I own a company that's building a green energy ranch outside of town."

"Oh," I said, thinking about the article I'd read in the paper. "I heard about the plans for that ranch. They did a huge write-up in the paper about it. It definitely sounds like a great idea."

"I hope so." He chuckled. "I'm putting a lot into it. It's been my dream since I was younger, and I just had to get to a place where I could afford to do it."

"Well, everyone in town is ecstatic about it," I said. "They're really looking forward to the opportunities it could provide for us."

"That's really great to hear," he said. "You never know with these kinds of things, especially next to small towns. Sometimes, they're excited, and sometimes, they come after you with torches and pitchforks."

"I don't think there'll be any rioting." I laughed. "The town thinks you're an angel that came to save them all."

A smirk crossed his lips, and I knew he had seen the perfect opportunity for a little bit of flirting. He laughed loudly at the angel comment and looked up at me, pinning me with a fiery stare. Heat blew through my chest, and I shuffled back and forth in my heels, feeling like my knees were going to give out on me.

"I'm definitely no angel," he said in a deep voice.

The look sent shivers down my spine, and the hair on the back of my neck stood up straight. He stood up off the hood and took a step toward me, his eyes dark. I swore for a second, he was going to kiss me, but maybe that was my wishful thinking.

"So, Emilia," he said with a grin. "When can I see you again? I mean for the date I paid five grand to have with you, of course."

"I don't know," I said, rolling my eyes. "That is some pretty hefty expectation on your end, sir. I just don't know how I am supposed to live up to five thousand dollars' worth of expectations. This town is only so big, and the fanciest restaurant we have has plastic tablecloths. You might just be in for a disappointment."

"I don't think disappointment is in the cards," he said. "Especially since I think you already lived up to the five grand's worth of expectations."

I smiled, looking down at the ground. I could feel my cheeks growing hotter, and I just knew my entire face was red. He was so damn sweet, and it was hard to take all at once. I gathered myself and looked back up at him.

"How about Friday night?" I said.

He smiled a big, toothy smile and looked back over his shoulder as his driver pulled up to the curb. I took his coat from my shoulders and handed it back to him. He hung it over his finger and then threw it over his shoulder, still staring me right in the eyes. He looked back at the black SUV waiting for him and then at me again.

"I'll pick you up on Friday," he said with charm.

He reached forward and cupped my cheek with his hand again, leaning forward and pressing his lips against the other one. I could smell his cologne, and the heat of his body made me shake in the knees. A shock of electricity jolted me at the touch of his lips, and it was unlike anything I had ever experienced before. Slowly, he pulled back and winked, turning and walking down to the SUV. I stood there unable to move until the car had disappeared around the corner. I shook my head and let out the air trapped in my lungs, turning and walking into the house. I hung my dress up in the closet, running my hand over the sequins one more time before pushing it to the back of the closet. From there, I jumped in the shower and let the hot water roll over me. I was still tingly from Lucas's kiss, and I sat there replaying it over and over again in my head. Where in the world did this guy come from?

Then, without warning, Janson's face popped back into my head. I shivered even under the hot water, thinking about his face staring down at me, that twitch under his eye going wild. He had come back into my life in the blink of an eye, and I hated everything about it. Just thinking about him made me sick to my stomach. I turned off the water and got out of the shower, drying myself off and climbing into bed. The last thing I wanted was for my last thoughts before sleep to be of Janson, so I pushed them out of my mind and tried to focus on looking forward to my upcoming date. I drifted off to sleep, knowing the rest of my week was going to be busy.

As the week progressed, I could still feel a confusion of emotions rolling around inside of me. I tried to focus on my work, pushing all that out, but it was almost impossible to do. I was really anticipating the date. I had already had an incredible time with Lucas, and it was only about ten minutes' worth. I knew if the date went anything like that ten minutes, I would have an amazing time. At the same time, my anxiety was rising almost as quickly. Janson had been out of my life for quite a while, and I had made sure of that by steering clear of anywhere he might be. Now that he had a taste of me again, though, he may not let it go. If he continued to pester me like that, he could make some serious problems for Lucas.

Lucas was a really sweet guy, and even though he had stepped in valiantly in the parking lot, he had no idea what Janson was capable of. Lucas was an innocent person in all of this and was not going to deserve the problems I knew Janson would cause him if we continued to be seen together. I knew I couldn't hide away from him forever, but the first time I really enjoyed another man's company ended up being because of Janson and that could severely backfire on both of us.

I spent Thursday afternoon at the horse rescue, doing some intermittent physical therapy, brushing their manes, and helping Alison clean out the barns. After a long afternoon there, I headed home and jumped in the shower to wash the smell of horse and manure off my skin. Even after all that time working with animals, I could still smell the pungent odor of my clothing when I got off work, which was probably a good thing. When I was done, I got out of the shower and wrapped my towel around me, wiping the fog from the mirror. I looked at my face in the reflection, catching some sort of movement in the windows behind me. I gasped and turned around, holding my towel tight against my chest.

Suddenly, I felt as if I were being watched. I looked back and forth, starting to panic. I grabbed my robe and threw it on before running to the windows, closing the blinds and making sure they were locked. A sound outside made me jump, and I ran to the door and pulled on it, making sure it, too, was secure. I went into the bedroom and sat down, rubbing my hands over my face. I was freaking out, and it was for no reason. It had to be stress, so I changed into my pajamas and went to bed, trying to keep my mind focused on other things.

When I woke up in the morning, I felt a bit better, so I got dressed for work and headed out. As I stepped down the stairs and turned toward my car, I shrieked, finding a dead cat laid out in front of the garage door. Chills ran up my spine at the sight of it. I covered my eyes and groaned, trying to shake the dark feeling out of my chest. I turned back around and bent down in front of the cat. It looked as if it had been hit by a car or possibly fallen and broken its neck. I shook my head and walked into the garage to grab a box. I kept telling myself there was nothing nefarious going on. It was just somebody who had brought it there knowing I was the vet, thinking they were doing the right thing. That had to be all it was. There was no reason for anyone else to do something that horrible to me.

I put the cat in a box and in the trunk of my car and headed toward work. I wanted to believe someone dropping the animal off was all it was, but in the back of my mind, there was something nagging at me, something telling me it was even more sinister than that. I reached down and turned on the music, not wanting to think about what that sinister thing might be. It was too much for me to handle.

My mood was off all day at work, that cat simmering in my mind. I tried to put it out of my mind by calling the mortuary and asking if she could bring the deceased animal over for proper disposal. Maybe if it were out of sight, it would be out of mind as well. After I dropped off the cat, I headed over to the stables to see Alison.

"Hey," I said, walking up.

"Hey, girl, did you drop the cat off?"

"Yeah," I sighed. "I just feel off from it, you know? I'm thinking about calling Lucas and canceling tonight."

"No, no, no," Alison said, walking over to me. "That cat was a coincidence. It was nothing creepy or anything like that. You need to go out and enjoy yourself. It might jolt you out of this mood."

"Maybe you're right." I smiled.

"Besides, he has to be a better date than Jimmy," she said, rolling her eyes. "He brought fried chicken from the gas station to the house last night and a copy of Days of Thunder. It was supposed to be a romantic movie night and dinner."

"Wow." I laughed. "That's ridiculous. He has no sense when it comes to that stuff."

"No, he doesn't." She smiled. "Anyway, go home, get a shower, and relax until your date."

"Yes, ma'am," I said, feeling better.

"Call me when it's over," she yelled after me.

I hoped it was as good as she thought it was going to be.

Chapter 7

Lucas

AS I RODE OVER TO PICK Emilia up from her house, I was quite surprised at how much I was looking forward to our date. My last couple of days in town had been rough, and this was a welcome reprieve. One of the city's councilmembers had stopped by the ranch to have a "conversation," or so he called it. From his stance to the way he spoke to me, I had started to get the impression the councilman's former warm welcome had quickly come to an end. It wasn't a good feeling at all, especially with so much work going into the ranch and everything being done on double time. Everything that needed to be discussed had been done months before my arrival, but suddenly, there were second thoughts. The councilman, out of nowhere, was discussing redoing the environmental impact survey, something we had not only done once but hired an outside firm of their choice to do a second time. It had taken us several months to complete, and we were all assured everything was on the up and up with it. There hadn't even been a peep about it until that moment.

As soon as he walked away, thinking I wasn't watching, he got on his cell phone. There was something fishy about the way he was acting, the way he slunk around. You could always tell when someone was being shady by the way they acted. You just had to open your eyes, and I had. Something strange was going on, and I needed to get to the bottom of it. There was no way I was going to let this project be pushed off even more than it already had been.

Needless to say, I needed to relax, rethink, and get my head on straight. Normally, that would include a weekend in my penthouse, doing research and drinking whiskey, but that wasn't in the cards. Emilia, on the other hand, was a very welcome distraction, someone who had taken my breath away while I was with her and stayed on mind ever since the night under the stars. I had been looking forward to seeing her since the moment I had left her in that driveway and gone back to the hotel. I pulled up in front of the small house and looked over at it, realizing it looked a lot different with light out than it had in the middle of the night. The yard was perfectly manicured, bushes lined under the windows, and it looked like it had been freshly painted not long before. It was the perfect house for the girl I had met, neat, petite, and pretty.

I jumped out of the car and looked at my hair in the window. I wanted to look nice but not overdone, so I had put on a pair of nice pants, a button-up shirt without a tie, and rolled up the sleeves. I headed up the walkway, glancing over in front of the garage at what looked like a stain of blood. I pulled my eyebrows together but figured it had to be spilled paint. I stood in front of the door and rang the doorbell. I could hear her walking toward the door, and I stood back and waited for her to open it. When she did, I could barely think. Emilia was so beautiful and took my breath away completely. She smiled at my reaction and blushed, looking down at the floor.

"You look beautiful." I smiled.

"Thank you," she said. "You too. Give me a second to grab my purse."

I watched her walk back to the kitchen and grab her bag off the counter. She was dressed more casually than my normal date would be dressed in New York City, but then again, the town only had two restaurants to choose from. Both of them were more of the casual eatery type of restaurants and nothing like the upscale bistro I would normally choose in the city. None of that mattered, though. I just wanted to be around her, to hear her talk, laugh, listen to her tell me about her life there in Bonanza. I found her to be more than fascinating, and I was curious about every part of her.

Her dress was actually perfect, both casual and nice at the same time. It was a simple navy-blue dress, dipping low in the front and hugging all her perfect curves. It was long, down to her calves, and she was wearing wedged heels with it. She looked stunning, even more so than she had when she was all dolled up in that blue sequined gown. Her makeup was simple but showed off her amazingly gorgeous face. Her hair cascaded over her shoulders, and it shimmered as she moved. She had definitely gotten my heart going fast. As she walked forward and leaned down to grab her keys off the side table, I couldn't help noticing how the V-neck of her dress showed a bountiful amount of her pale skin. It looked like she would feel like silk if I touched her, and every part of me wanted to touch her. My cock was throbbing in my pants, but I had to restrain myself, remembering that this was a date and not an excuse for me to grope a beautiful woman before we even got out the door.

She smiled and turned to lock the front door. I hustled back to the SUV and opened the passenger door, standing slightly behind it to hide the fact that my pants had become incredibly tight, and I was trying to get my hard-on to rescind. It was crazy to me how much she had already turned me on. I wanted to take her inside right then and have my way with her. I shook the thoughts from my head and closed her door, going around and climbing into the driver's seat.

"No driver tonight?"

"I wanted it to just be us." I smiled. "I have to say, though, I'm not used to there being no traffic whatsoever."

"I keep forgetting you're from New York City." She laughed. "I don't think I could deal with the number of people there."

"You get used to it." I smiled.

The drive to the restaurant was short, and we were there within five minutes. I had decided to take her to the Mexican restaurant in town since it was some of my favorite food, and I had heard it was to die for on the West Coast. I parked the car and helped her out, draping her hand over my arm and opening the door for her. It was a small place and pretty empty for a Friday night, but I figured that was for the best. We wouldn't be distracted by anyone else. The host showed us to a booth in the back, and I slid in across from her, smiling as I took the menu. We both got a margarita and perused the menu, snacking on the chips and salsa. When the waiter returned, we ordered and then sat back, just looking at each other.

"Tell me about yourself." She smiled. "You're the mystery man in town."

"I am, aren't I?" I laughed. "I grew up in New York City with my mother and father. I was a pretty strange kid, one person to everyone else and another behind closed doors."

"Wasn't everyone?" She laughed.

"True, very true." I smiled. "I focused on learning as much about computers as I could, and then, I would hide my nerdy math side from my friends. They didn't really like smart kids, so I played it off."

"I was the opposite." She laughed. "But it wasn't computers, for sure."

"There was just something about computers that spoke to me," I said. "The programming languages just made sense to me. So, when I graduated from high school, I skipped college and started to build a series of computer apps before apps were on everything, of course. Think back before cell phones really surfed the internet unless it was an emergency."

"Okay." She smiled, eating a chip. "So, you were ahead of your time."

"Eh," I said, tilting my head back and forth. "In the public's perception maybe, but in the computer world, I was right on time. So, anyway, when the apps were done, I sold a couple of them to small, technology companies, and the others I used myself to build an income on the side. It was a way for me to do what I loved, work toward the future and not have to spend my time, I don't know, working on cars or something to make money. I wasn't the guy who could see himself doing something like that. I made enough to pay my rent but not much more than that."

"Okay," she said. "That sounds really awesome. I remember waitressing as my first job, hating every single moment of it."

"I can see you as a New York waitress with that sass but not out here." I laughed.

"So how did you go from a couple small apps to where you are now?"

"Well, a few years ago, I developed an algorithm that better prioritized ads online. It stuck to personal preferences for the viewer, so more ads were making companies more money. I ended up selling that to one specific social media site for the highest individual acquisition in history. It was just me, sitting in front of these computer geniuses, selling them something they had never been able to come up with on their own. It's still one of my finest moments."

"Holy crap," she said with wide eyes. "I can't even imagine doing something like that. That's amazing."

"Since then, I've concentrated all my efforts on building an empire." I shrugged. "I want a company that's viable and profitable but at the same time mean something. I don't want to make rubber stoppers for drains. I want diversity in what we do, and I want it to be on the cutting edge of technology."

I knew I wasn't telling her the whole truth, but I wasn't ready to tell her any of the dark stuff from the past. She was interested, though, asking some really good questions. She seemed like she really wanted to know who I was and where I came from. It was refreshing since most women in the city just wanted to know how much money I made.

"So, what's after the ranch?"

"We have some things working, all in the energy field." I smiled. "But you know what? I feel like an asshole."

"Why?" She laughed.

"Because I have this beautiful, mysterious, interesting woman sitting in front of me, and I've been doing nothing but monopolizing the entire conversation," I said.

"I don't know about mysterious, interesting, or even beautiful, but I'm enjoying hearing about your life."

I smiled. "And I want to hear about yours. Tell me about you. I want to know everything."

Chapter 8

Emilia

I LOOKED ACROSS THE table at that handsome man sitting across from me, and I couldn't help but think about how much I was enjoying my dinner with him. In fact, I was enjoying it a lot more than I thought I would. I really had figured I would be there, but my mind would be back on the cat in my driveway, but he took all of that away, quieting my mind and giving me something much happier to focus on. Lucas was such an interesting guy. He had so many different layers to him, nothing like I thought a rich guy from New York City would be like. He was really grounded, really down to earth, and it was refreshing. I admired his life and how he'd built his own fortune through hard work and patience, not by anyone handing him anything. I had met people who were rich because their family was rich, not because they'd earned it, and they never appreciated the small things in life. They were always looking toward the bigger items, the shopping, the money, not the accomplishments and hard work it took to get there.

"So, what's after the ranch?" I asked.

"We have some things working, all in the energy field." He smiled. "But you know what? I feel like an asshole."

"Why?" I laughed.

"Because I have this beautiful, mysterious, interesting woman sitting in front of me and I have been doing nothing but monopolizing the entire conversation," he said.

"I don't know about mysterious, interesting, or even beautiful, but I'm enjoying hearing about your life." I laughed.

He smiled. "And I want to hear about yours. Tell me about you. I want to know everything."

When he asked me about my life, I suddenly felt so shy. He had done so much, conquered the world, built big things, created technologies that changed the way we viewed our computers. I had done pretty much nothing compared to him, and I felt like any attempt to make my life seem anything but ordinary would be futile. I knew he wasn't going to let me out of it, though. He wanted to know about me and my little life.

"Well," I said, sighing deeply. "My life is nowhere near as exciting as yours has been. I can promise you that."

"That's a good thing." He smiled. "Tell me."

"I grew up right here in Bonanza," I said. "I lived on my parents' dairy farm on the other side of town, played with cows, ran around with my best friend, Alison. I knew I wanted to be a vet as long as I could remember, so I went to a school right outside of town and then built up my vet business here in Bonanza. There wasn't another vet within fifty miles, so I knew we needed one here. When it was up and running and I had moved into my house, my parents closed the farm and retired to Phoenix."

I felt completely and utterly boring compared to his story. There was nothing exciting about my life unless you counted the surprise cow births or doing surgery on a horse. Other than that, it was just me and the animals.

"What kind of animals do you work on?"

"All kinds," I said. "Well, almost. I don't have the education for exotic pets, but I can figure it out if I need to. I work with a lot of large farm animals and then your run-of-the-mill dogs and cats."

"That sounds really cool to be able to help animals like that," he said. "Very rewarding. I'm hoping I find that kind of satisfaction in my work, you know? The kind that makes you feel good when you go to bed because you helped someone or something."

He was charming and sweet and did everything he could to dig deeper. I was flattered at the fact that he was so interested in knowing about me. There weren't many eligible men in Bonanza, and the ones who were, really had no clue. When dinner was done, he paid the bill and smiled over at me.

"Let's take a walk, and you can show me around downtown," he said.

"All right," I said. "But only if you have about, uhm, five or so minutes to see everything."

"I think I can spare the time." He laughed.

We walked out of the building and across the street, taking the sidewalk downtown. The entire time, he cracked small town jokes, making me laugh until my stomach hurt. I really liked being around him. It was like opening my eyes for the first time.

"Have you ever been to New York City?" he asked as we strolled along.

"The Big Apple? No." I chuckled. "Honestly, the biggest city I've ever been to is Portland, and I really didn't like it that much. Have you been to Portland?"

"No," he said. "But I've been to Seattle, which was interesting. I went to the fish market and to the first Starbucks and ate some fries from a food truck. That was about the extent of it, but it was worlds away from New York City."

"Yeah? What is New York like?"

"Busy, crowded, crazy all the time." He chuckled. "But so beautiful. There's the Statue of Liberty, the 9/11 Memorial, the park, the boroughs, and so many different shops and restaurants. The ethnicity diversity in the city is amazing. You can go one block down and have the best Irish food you've ever had outside of Ireland itself and then turn the corner and eat a scone that will change your life."

"Wow, life-changing scones." I laughed. "It sounds really amazing. It does. I just don't think I could see myself there."

"I think you'd be surprised when you got there," he said. "I think you would fit right in."

"Maybe, or maybe I would get lost and never find my way home." I chuckled. "I'm a small-town girl, born and raised on the farm, knowing everyone's names, going to a million weddings and even more funerals. Going to town carnivals and seeing the lights twinkle at the tree lighting ceremony in the winter. In a way, I think small town is bred in me. I have imagined living in those places, but I know in my heart, I would always miss this, you know?"

"I don't, but I think I can relate in some ways." He smiled.

We walked back to the restaurant, and he helped me into the SUV, smiling as he closed the door behind me. I watched as he hustled around to the driver's side and climbed in. He was so handsome all the time, and it was amazing to me how good of a time I was having. He sat there for a second, looking down the empty street, turning to me and grabbing my hand. Tingles of excitement blew through me as he started the car and headed back to my house. The drive home didn't take long at all, and I found myself wishing I lived much farther away. I wasn't ready to say good night to him. I honestly felt like I could sit there and talk to him all night out under the stars. We knew nothing about each other, which never happened in a small town like this. It was invigorating getting to know someone like this, finding out all their secrets, all the things that made them tick. The memories someone pointed out in the beginning were always good indicators of what kind of person they were.

The car pulled down my street and toward the house, the lights passing over the other houses. As he pulled up in front, the headlights shone brightly on the garage. I froze, dropping his hand and sitting forward, staring at the driveway. There was something on the ground between my car and the garage door, something that looked like it was once alive. I blinked, feeling him looking over at me.

"What's wrong?"

"There's something on the ground in front of the garage," I said. "I can't tell what it is, but I think it's an animal of some kind."

He leaned over and looked at the mound on the ground, leaning back in his chair. I turned and looked at him, a frown covering my face. Not again. This couldn't be happening again.

"You stay here," he said. "I'm going to go check it out."

He got out and ran toward the house, stopping a few feet from the animal. I slowly got out of the car and walked up behind him, seeing a fawn lying in the driveway, its throat cut, blood trickling down the driveway. I put my hands over my mouth and gasped. Lucas turned around and stood in front of me, staring into my tear-filled eyes. He forced me to look at him, grabbing me by the shoulders and bending his head down to my level.

"I want you to go inside and lock the door," he said. "I'm going to take care of this, okay? When I'm done, I'll walk around back to make sure I don't see anything unusual, and then, I'll knock on the back door. I want you to go inside, though. You don't need to be out here for this."

I shook my head, tears beginning to stream down my face. I didn't understand what was happening or why anyone would do something like this. It was a baby and obviously had not died from an accident or from natural causes. Someone had killed that poor baby and dumped it in front of my garage, right where the cat had been. I looked up at Lucas and opened my mouth to protest, but he shook his head.

"I'm serious," he said in a low, calm voice. "I want you to go inside and let me take care of this, okay?"

I nodded and walked to the front door. I searched through my purse, finding my keys and pulling them out. I grabbed them with both hands, trying to steady them from shaking. I got the key inside, opened the door, and quickly shut it behind me. I locked both locks and leaned my back against it, sobbing into my hands. Who could have done something so terrible like that? I took in a deep breath and leaned my head back, wiping the tears from my face. I needed to get myself under control. I couldn't lose it just because there was a man there to protect me.

I walked down the hall, turning on all the lights in the house and grabbing the teapot. I filled it with water, watching my hands still shaking, and put it on the stove. I needed some nice, warm tea, something that would help calm my nerves and help me get my emotions under control. As the water heated, I pulled down two mugs and the teabags, deciding on English Breakfast. I prepared the cups with sugar and the bags and waited for the water to boil. I looked toward the back door, wondering what could be taking Lucas so long. He'd told me to stay in the house, and that was what I was going to do until something forced me otherwise. As the teapot began to scream, I picked it up and poured the hot water into the mugs, setting it back down on a cool burner.

I turned to grab a spoon from the center island and screamed, grabbing my chest. Lucas was standing at the back door looking in, and I must not have heard him knock with the teapot going off. I walked over and unlocked the door, letting him inside and locking it behind him. This night was going to get the best of me yet.

Chapter 9

Lucas

I TOOK SOME TRASH BAGS from Emilia's garage and wrapped the fawn up tightly before putting it in the back of the SUV. I walked around the front yard looking for any kind of clue as to why someone would have done this. I had never seen a dead deer in person before, and it made me sad to have to wrap it up. There were a bunch of local guys working on the ranch now, and I knew one of them would be able to tell me how to dispose of it. I hoped one of them would take it and maybe even give me some idea why someone had killed it. It was just a baby, and this couldn't possibly be legal when it came to hunting, not that I knew that much about the sport. Either way, I had to get rid of the thing for Emilia. There was no way that she needed to deal with something like this.

I walked around to the backyard and poked my head in the small shed, just making sure there was no one around hiding. When I felt comfortable enough, I turned, walking back toward the house. I didn't want to be gone too long. I knew that Emilia didn't need to be alone. I wanted to focus on her, help her through this. She was incredibly upset, and I didn't blame her one bit. Anyone would have been upset by it, and there was no way that fawn wandered into her yard and was injured like that by accident. Emilia had spent her entire life learning about animals, taking care of them, nursing them back to health and everything in between. She loved animals more than she loved people. I could tell by the way she talked about her job. Seeing a dead one, one that was so young and obviously killed on purpose had to be no fun for her, and I couldn't imagine how she might be feeling.

I stepped up to the door and knocked, hearing the sound of a teapot and seeing her standing with her back to me. I waited, finding it pointless to keep banging when she couldn't hear me. As she turned around, though, she jumped straight into the air, grabbing her chest. I smiled and waved at her, making sure she knew it was me. She shook her head and walked over, opening the door and letting me in. I walked into her kitchen and watched as she closed and locked the door.

"Are you okay?" I asked.

"No," she said. "But I will survive it. That poor baby deer. I just don't understand."

"Me either," I said.

"Would you like some tea?"

"I'd love some," I replied.

She grabbed the mugs off the counter, walked over to the kitchen table, and sat down. I sat next to her, turning my chair toward her to talk. I needed to know what was going on, what she thought might be the motive for someone dropping off a dead animal in her driveway. She took a sip of her tea and put the mug down, looking over at me. I took her hands in mine and smiled at her sweetly.

"Do you have any idea what might have happened?" I asked. "How that animal might have ended up in your driveway?"

"I don't know." She sighed. "This morning, when I got up to go to work, there was a dead cat in the driveway. It spooked me at first, but when I took a closer look, it seemed as if it had maybe been hit by a car or fallen and broken its neck. It certainly didn't look like that deer, which was obviously killed by someone and brutally."

"What did you do with the cat?"

"I took it to the mortuary and had it disposed of," she said.

"Do you know why someone would leave the cat there?"

"I don't know," she said. "I figured maybe someone from the community, someone who knew I was the only vet in town, put it there. Maybe they thought they were somehow helping by bringing the dead animal to my home so they wouldn't just rot in the street or something. I thought it could have been someone's pet, or someone hit the cat and didn't know what to do so they brought it to my house. People here in this town try to do the right thing, even though sometimes they're misguided in their attempts."

"Right," I said, leaning back in my chair. "I can see how you would think that with the cat."

"The deer is strange, I know," she said, shaking her head. "It doesn't look like it was accidentally killed, but you never know what happened."

"True," I said, shaking my head.

I wanted to believe Emilia's theory was the truth. It would be simple, non-threatening, and could be handled with a call to the mayor or to the paper to let people know how to properly dispose of animals. It was also a little far-fetched, and I found it hard to believe that was what was going on. Truth be told, my gut was telling me something else might be at play, something that had more to do with the message behind the dead animals than someone trying to help out. My mind immediately went to the other night when I'd first met Emilia and to the confrontation she'd had with the sheriff. I had to wonder if he had something to do with what was going on. My first impression of the man made me think there was a very real possibility he'd had something to do with it, but I couldn't know for sure without knowing more about his relationship with Emilia, something I wasn't sure she wanted to talk to me about.

We sat for several moments in the quiet, and I watched her stare blankly out the back door window as she sipped her tea. I still felt like I needed to protect her, and I couldn't let some simple questions get in the way of that. I needed to ask her about the sheriff.

"Emilia, I think you know I could tell there was more to the incident with the sheriff in the parking lot than him losing a bid," I said carefully. "I'd really like to know what kind of relationship the two of you had."

"No," she said, shaking her head. "The past needs to stay in the past. Digging that kind of stuff up can only lead to bad things, and I'm one person who thinks looking to the past can only be harmful to the future. I just want my past to stay dead and buried, Lucas. I don't want to think about it anymore."

"I understand," he said. "I have things like that in my past. And I agree it's usually best to leave the past right there and move forward. However, after seeing how the sheriff reacted to you and me in the parking lot the other night, I can't help but think ..."

"What?" she said, looking at me. "You can't help but think what?"

"That maybe he doesn't see you as part of his past," I said. "Maybe he still sees you as part of his present and part of his future. This is a small town, and there's no way he didn't know about our date tonight."

"Dammit." She frowned and rubbed her face. "I don't want anything to do with that man. He's really not a good person. That night in the parking lot was a fluke. I've stayed away from him for a very long time."

"Why?" I said. "You can trust me. I'm just trying to help."

"Fine," she said after a few moments. "I'll tell you about the sheriff and me, but first you have to tell me about your exes or at least the last one you had."

As soon as she said that, a wave of anxiety ran through my chest. I'd been trying to keep things about myself on a positive note all night long, but as with most exes, there was never a good story behind it. I wanted to let her in, I really did, but at the same time, I still wanted her to see me in a positive light. There were things from my past, things about me, that I wanted to keep hidden, and it wasn't for any other reason than that I wasn't the same man I used to be. My last relationship hadn't ended well at all, not even in the least. It was a complicated story with twists and turns, and in the end, I would come out looking like the worst out of the two of us. I really didn't want to tell Emilia about it, not yet at least. I wanted her to continue to see the man I was, not the man I used to be, but if I told her everything, she wouldn't be able to stop herself from seeing that man. I twisted my hands together and looked down at the floor, trying to decide what to say next.

I might not want to reveal my past but neither did she. I needed to know what had happened between the sheriff and Emilia. It was a burning need in my gut. It mostly had to do with my suspicion that he was somehow involved in the animals being left in the driveway, but it also had to do with my protective urges toward Emilia. I couldn't explain why, but I no longer just wanted to keep her safe. I felt like I had to keep her safe from the sheriff and everyone else. The only way to get her to open up was by telling her about my ex or at least most of it.

"All right," I said, sitting up. "My last relationship didn't end long ago. I was dating a girl named Mia, who I had met at one of my technology convention dinners. She was the daughter of a very wealthy and very powerful man who did business with my company and many others throughout the world. She was used to a life of luxury and privilege. It was just how she was raised, and it was the only way she ever knew. Her father was extremely controlling over her, watching her every move, scrutinizing every man she ever dated, and basically pulling the purse strings, which, in her life, controlled everything else. This upset her. She wanted freedom from that but didn't want to give up the life she was accustomed to. So, she started dating me to piss off her father. He didn't like my past."

"Your past?" Emilia asked.

"I grew up poor, with very little, and had to work for everything I had from the time I was a kid," I said. "I didn't come from any sort of money at all. Her father didn't care what kind of money I had now. He wanted Mia to marry into a rich family dynasty. He wanted her to be part of a family with old money like his family was. The last thing he wanted was a guy who had built himself up from the bottom and still thought like a poor guy. Don't get me wrong. I have really nice things, but I don't think like the rich people do. I don't have an air to me, and I don't look down on others because they aren't rich."

"I can see that," she said, listening to my story. "You've come off as very down-to-earth since I met you."

"I am down-to-earth." I smiled. "I don't want to be the guy who raises a family with a silver spoon in their mouths. I came from nothing, and I've seen how quickly you can go back to that. I will never take that for granted. Anyway, she got tired of the game, and after quite a while, she dumped me."

For a moment, I felt guilty about only having told her a slice of the real story. The look on her face was of sincere sympathy, and that was what triggered the guilt. In reality, the story had so many more pieces, but I wasn't ready to let her know about the man I used to be.

Chapter 10

Emilia

HE LOOKED UP AT ME and nodded, having told me his story. I realized then that it was my turn to talk, and I really didn't want to, but he had held up his end of the bargain, so it was only right. I cleared my throat and leaned back in the chair, looking out the window.

"Janson and I had been dating for about three years," I said, starting the story. "There was even a period of time when his house was under renovation that he'd moved in here with me. It was a very short time since we both found that living together wasn't quite the easiest thing to do. I'd always had this suspicion that he was cheating on me and even had several people in town come and tell me, but it took quite a while before I had hard evidence to really show him. One day when I was at the station visiting him for lunch, I saw some texts come in on his phone from a waitress at the saloon downtown. She was talking about the night before and all kinds of personal things, things only someone who had slept with him would know. I left the station and went home and thought about it until he came over that evening. I confronted him, and when he admitted to it, I broke it off with him. It's been a while but really not that long if I think about it. About six months maybe."

"And how did he take it?" Lucas asked.

"Not very good." I smiled. "Let's just say he was not happy about it, and he let me know that very sternly. I stayed away from him after that, until the other night in the parking lot."

I turned back in my chair and drank the last of my tea, not wanting to look him in the eyes. I had left out the worst part of the abuse. I didn't want Lucas to feel sorry for me. It drove me nuts when anyone felt sorry for me, much less the guy I was really starting to like. It wasn't something I had told anyone but Alison, and it needed to stay that way. It wasn't like I could go to the police. He was the sheriff.

I looked over at Lucas as he sat thinking about what I said. I realized in that moment that me not telling him about the abuse was more than just me not wanting him to feel sorry for me. I wanted him to respect me, not pity me, not want to feel bad for me. I wanted him to think of me as a strong person.

I shook my head and pushed my chair back, taking the cups over to the sink to rinse them off. I was tired of living in this fear of Janson, this creepy shadow who seemed to follow me everywhere. It wasn't that I was stuck in the past. It was that the past was always right there in front of me, chasing me around every corner. I couldn't get away from him unless I moved, and Bonanza was my home. I still had the hope that he would one day move past it all and leave me alone. I knew it was a long shot, but I had to hope for something more than the life I was living.

I finished rinsing the mugs and put them in the dishwasher, closing it and drying off my hands. When I turned back around, I found Lucas standing behind me, leaning against the center island. He was looking down at his hands, thinking about something, so I stood there waiting for him to talk.

"I want to ask you something," he said.

"All right," I said, nodding my head. "I'll answer the best I can."

"Does Janson still want you?" he asked. "I mean is he still in love with you like he was six months ago?"

I stared at him for a minute before dropping my eyes to the floor, nodding my head up and down. I didn't want to say the words out loud because I hated the thought of Janson. I hated the thought of him even thinking about me, much less still being in love with me. The man had hurt me in ways I didn't know would ever heal. I turned my head and looked off into the distance. My thoughts whirled around in my head, knowing exactly where Lucas was going with all of this. He thought

Janson might have something to do with the animals out front, and sadly, I couldn't deny it was a possibility. He had never done something like this before, but that didn't mean he wasn't capable.

Lucas reached over and put his finger under my chin, guiding my gaze back to his. I could tell by the look in his eyes that he wanted to know more, that he needed to know more, but I didn't want to tell him. He could sense I was holding back, and he had seen the way Janson had treated me that day. There was no way I could deny that he had done that before and more than once. So, to head off any more questions, I took in a deep breath and lunged forward, pressing my lips against his. He stumbled backward, catching himself on the island counter. I had caught him off guard, but he had done the same to me when I felt just how soft his lips really were. In fact, he had caught me off guard from the first moment I met him.

I stepped forward, following him backward, unable to pull my lips from his. He tasted like honey and tea, and the scent of his cologne wafted strongly into my brain. When he had gotten his footing, he immediately responded, wrapping his arms around my body and pulling me close to him. I wound my arms up around his neck as he deepened the kiss, moving his tongue over my lips and pushing them apart. It had been a long time since a man had kissed me like that, and I found a small whimper escaping my throat. The intensity between us took my breath away, and I could feel myself getting weak in the knees. The lust and desire between us were as thick as fog, and finding a way out of that embrace was nowhere even close to my thoughts. I didn't know if it was the moment or if it was the attraction, but the man had completely swept me off my feet.

Things quickly started to heat faster and faster until we were so close together, I could barely breathe. I could feel the bulge in his pants pressing against my body, and in that moment, I wanted nothing more than for him to take me right there in the kitchen. I hadn't felt this kind of attraction ever in my life, like we were two magnets being pulled closer together by the second. It had been simmering since the beginning, but until my lips hit his, I'd had no idea how intense it really was. I wasn't the kind of girl who jumped into bed with a man right away, but Lucas made me want to throw caution to the wind. I had to fight it, though. There was more at stake than just my love life. If Lucas was right, him being there with me was bad for him and bad for me. He had no idea what kind of pull Janson had in that town.

Finally, I mustered enough strength to pull myself away, dislodging his arms from around my body. Instantly, I regretted it, wanting to be right back there pressed against him, but I needed to have more self-control than that. I leaned back against the counter and put my hand out, both of us out of breath. We stood there for several moments collecting ourselves. I looked up at him as he pulled away from the island and took a step forward. His eyes moved up my body and met mine, turning dark with lust. I couldn't look at him any longer, knowing I was teetering on the edge of self-control. I looked away quickly, closing my eyes and breathing deeply, trying to gain control of myself. This man had a serious spell over me, and as much as I liked it, I had to break it, at least for that night.

"You all right?" he asked.

"Yeah," I said, nodding my head and wiping my lips. "I'm all right. A little tired is all. It's been a really long day with work and the stables and then the date and the deer. I'm pretty much spent."

"I understand." He smiled. "I can take the hint."

"No," I said, turning around. "Please, don't take it in a bad way."

"Hey," he whispered. "It's okay. We can maybe pick this conversation up later."

"I'd like that." I smiled, looking down at the floor.

"I gotta get going anyway. I have some phone conferences really early in the morning." He smiled, grabbing his keys off the table and turning back to me. "I want you to know that I had a really lovely evening with you. It's definitely climbing the charts as one of the best dates I've ever had. Thank you for that. It was definitely unexpected. You were unexpected."

"You too." I smiled. "But I have to ask, was it worth five thousand dollars?"

He chuckled and walked out of the kitchen and down to the front door. I stood there at the front door watching him open it and turn back toward me. His smile sent butterflies through my whole body, and my knees went weak watching him.

"Honestly?" he said. "I should have paid double."

With that, he winked and walked out of the house, closing the door behind him. I smiled, walking over and locking the door, leaning against it and laughing to myself. I really knew how to get myself into some crazy situations, including falling for some guy I barely knew but seemed to have a knack for saving me every chance he got. He definitely was going to be on my mind for a very long time.

That night, I tossed and turned in my bed, my body still on fire as I lay there thinking about how hot that kiss was. His lips, his smell, the feeling of his bulge pressing against me, it all ran wildly through my mind as I tried to sleep. Even in my dreams, I could see him standing in the rain, kissing me passionately. He was shirtless, his skin slick from the rain falling over us. Every drop of rain that hit me instantly turned to steam, sizzling and radiating off my body because I was so turned on. I woke over and over, wanting to fall asleep again, wanting to see him in my dreams and touch that soft, supple skin. I barely got a wink of sleep that night, and I was okay with that.

Chapter 11

Lucas

IT WAS NO USE. I COULDN'T stop thinking about Emilia all night. I tossed and turned, got up and walked around, showered and tried again, but there was just no way I could stop thinking about her. That kiss, everything about it, had driven me to complete distraction. The way her lips moved across mine, the way her body shaped against me, it was all so perfect and probably the biggest turn-on I had ever experienced. My mind wouldn't let it go and neither could my body for that matter. I didn't think I had ever had that passionate and lustful of a connection with anyone in my life, and it just happened to be while I was on assignment far away from New York City. It was my luck all wrapped up in a very telling package.

When I woke up the next morning, or more like rolled over and looked at the clock, I decided a little time out at the ranch would do me some good. Sure, it was Saturday, but we had some serious deadlines going on, and this wasn't supposed to be a vacation. It was supposed to be work toward the project I had been planning for years. I had paid for unlimited overtime to get the ranch up and running as quickly as possible, so I knew the planning team would be there, working hard. The guys I had hired were serious about the job, thankful to have one, and even more thankful I was paying higher than average wages with time and a half. All I wanted to see was good quality progress, and I was happy. Besides, I figured getting to work would help me take my mind off the enchanting veterinarian who was running through it even as I sat there getting ready to leave.

When I had prepared for the date the day before, I had been a bit nervous, but it was nothing more than first-date jitters. There was no doubt in mind, after spending ten minutes with her before, that we would have a great time on our date. What I wasn't prepared for was how good of a time I'd had, minus the dead deer of course. Sure, I was attracted to her. I had been attracted from the moment she'd walked out onto the auction stage wearing that sequined blue dress, but this was more. Our attraction wasn't only off the charts, but I hadn't expected our personalities to mesh so well together. I seriously could have sat at that restaurant for the rest of my life and never gotten bored talking to her. Talk about firsts. That was definitely one for me.

I wish I could say we seemed to be perfectly matched and were all good to go, but we weren't. This girl was a small-town vet, a girl who loved Bonanza and loved the idea of small-town living. I, on the other hand, was only going to be in town for another week, tops, before heading back to a completely different world in the concrete jungles of New York City where if you knew your neighbor's first name, you were doing good. It was obvious those facts alone were a red flag to me. I shouldn't pursue her or anything with her any further. It was a recipe for heartache, and I was starting to think it would be on both of our parts. I would just need to change my mindset about the whole thing. I could chalk it up to an enjoyable charity auction date, a great donation to a very deserving organization, and let that be that. The feelings would simmer out eventually, and I would move on, or at least I hoped so.

I walked out of the bathroom and sat down on the edge of the bed, grabbing my boots and putting them on. The site was a pretty dusty place, and with recent rains, it would probably still be muddy. It was nice to hang up my suit and tie for something more casual for once. I wondered if Emilia would prefer me in jeans and boots or in a suit and tie, realizing again that she had crept back into my mind. I shook the thoughts and grabbed my keys, deciding to drive myself that day. I jumped into the SUV and headed toward the site. As I was driving, my phone started to buzz, so I patched the call through to the Bluetooth in the SUV and answered the call.

"Brother," Alec said, laughing. "I was hoping I'd catch you!"

It was my best friend, Alec, who was still in New York tending to his own billion-dollar company. Alec was the guy who always gave me good advice, always steered me in the right direction, and never let me down when it came to being there at the perfect moment. Most of the time, I wouldn't survive my life without having him to lean on.

"Hey, dude." I smiled.

"I was just calling to see how the project was going," he said.

"Oh, man, it's going well. It's coming together nicely minus a little snafu with one of the councilmen, but I'm sure it'll blow over," I said. "This town, though, is literally the smallest town I have ever seen. You could throw a rock from one end to the other, and the population is around five hundred."

"Shit, dude, I think my preschool graduating class had five hundred kids in it." He laughed. "I think there were three times that many people at the last gala you held."

"I know, right?" I laughed. "The sheriff here even walks around with a badge pinned to his leather jacket."

"So, I'm assuming it's safe to say you're dying of boredom." He laughed.

"I would be if it weren't for this little, sexy town vet who's been keeping me occupied." I smirked.

"I should have known you would have found the one hot chick out of the bunch and bagged her." He laughed.

"Not yet," I said in defense. "We went on a date, and it was pretty amazing. But I'm debating on whether to see her again since I'm leaving in a week, and she's actually, genuinely, a nice girl."

"Personally, I think you should call it quits on that little venture," he said. "You tend to break hearts even when you aren't trying to. And you know how quickly girls get attached to you. It's like you give off some crazy pheromone or something."

"I know," I groaned. "I actually like this chick for once, like really dig her. She's been on my mind since I met her."

"Let me put a name out there for you and see if it rings any bells," he said. "Natasha."

I groaned just hearing the name, shaking my head while I drove. He had to bring up Natasha, which always set me straight. I sighed and turned into the drive for the site.

"If you don't want to hurt the girl, you should stop seeing her now," he said.

"You're right," I said. "But, hey, I'm at the site. I'll call you later."

"Will do, buddy," he said.

I parked the car and got out, not giving myself any time to think. I went straight to work checking on the progress and lending a hand wherever I could. Later that afternoon, one of the workers came in my office and reported an elk who was limping around the tree line.

"You sure?" I said.

"Yes, sir," he replied. "Seen them all my life, but this one is acting funny."

"All right." I put down my clipboard and headed outside.

I followed the worker to the edge of the property and looked over at the tree line. Sure enough, there was an elk standing there, but it was more than limping. It looked very injured, almost so much that it could barely walk. My heart went out for the thing, and thoughts of the deer in the back of my SUV made me think of Emilia. She was a vet. Maybe she could help the poor guy. I knew I was supposed to be staying away from Emilia, but I couldn't help myself. There was an injured animal near my property, and I couldn't just let that go. Before I even realized what I was doing, I had my phone out and I was dialing Emilia, hoping she was going to be available to help. She answered after only two rings.

"Hey there," she said. "Miss me already?"

"You could say that." I laughed, butterflies shooting up into my stomach.

"What's up? You just calling to talk, or is there something going on?" she asked.

"Well, I heard you make house calls," I said, watching the elk trying to move but bending down on its front legs and lying on the ground instead.

I never knew my heart could break for animals like it had with the fawn and with this elk. I was starting to think this town was making me soft, but I was okay with that. Emilia laughed on the other end of the line.

"I make house calls but for animals." She chuckled. "I'm not really sure you qualify for what I do. What's going on?"

"There's an elk on the edge of the property, and it's injured," I said. "It's barely able to walk. In fact, it just laid down in the brush and is snorting and making a strange noise like it's in pain."

"Oh," she said, her tone instantly going serious. "Don't approach it. Injured animals can be dangerous if you don't handle them correctly. I'm going to throw my stuff in the truck and head over from the stables."

"Thanks," I said, staring over at the field. After I got off the phone, I looked over at my ranch worker. "I have a vet on her way. Oh, hey, while we're on the subject of wildlife, I have a dead deer in the back of my car. It was left in the vet's driveway for some reason. You think you could dispose of it for me?"

"Sure," he said, looking at me strangely. "Kind of strange a deer would wander out that far."

"Yeah, I thought that too," I said, turning and walking back over to the parking area.

Emilia arrived shortly afterward, and as soon as I saw her, my heart began to race. I walked her over to the edge of the field and pointed toward the woods, showing her the elk. It was lying completely down, not even flinching as we stood there. I could tell by the look on her face that she was already trying to figure out what was wrong.

"I'm going to approach," she said. "But these animals are wild and spook very easily, which causes them to kick out pretty hard. I want you to stay back, okay?"

"All right," I said, nodding my head.

I walked halfway with her and stopped, letting her proceed the rest of the way on her own. I watched in awe as she slowly crept toward the animal, setting her bag down and kneeling just out of its reach. The tone of her voice was calm and sweet, and the animal responded to her like it knew her. It was amazing to watch, like she had a connection with the animal that I couldn't understand. I watched as she carefully pulled each leg up and inspected its hooves. The animal barely moved, only shaking its head from time to time. When she was done, she moved away as carefully as when she had approached until she returned back at my side.

"How is it?" I said.

"She has something lodged in her hoof," she said. "I need a tool from the back of the van."

"Okay," I said, turning with her.

We walked across the field and back to her work van with the name of her vet clinic on the side of it. I was impressed with how prepared she was for a hometown operation. She opened the back and grabbed a couple of things out of the bags she had stowed there. The van was neat but cramped, and I could tell she was getting a bit frustrated. She opened another bag and started digging around.

"This isn't the ideal situation," she said, looking over her shoulder. "One day, I want to buy an even larger van and create a mobile lab in the back of it. Kind of like an ambulance, only I can do a lot of things right there on the spot. It will make treating animals on house calls so much easier."

I watched her sift through her things, pulling out the tools she would need. It was the first time I had seen her in action on the job, and she was really good at it. I admired her for that, for how focused she was, and how devoted she was to her job and to the animal. She smiled at me and turned back, walking back out to the edge. I followed her and stopped where I was before, watching her approach the elk and kneel down in front of it. She started to treat the animal carefully, and after a few minutes, the elk jumped to its feet and ran off into the forest. I could feel a warmth in my chest, watching her smile, and I realized that when she was happy, so was I.

Chapter 12

Emilia

AFTER THE ANIMAL HAD run off, I walked with Lucas back to the van and threw my tools into the back. He walked me inside and started giving me a small tour of the main building, stopping at the office he had been using. The place was coming along really well and really fast. I was impressed with the work he'd been doing and with how much money he was pumping into the community. The office was functional and nothing more. It wasn't fancy or ornate and seemed to fit the purpose. For a billionaire, Lucas sure did seem to have simple tastes, which I liked. I wasn't the kind of girl who was into the fancy and crazy. I could only imagine how hard it would be for someone to go from New York City billionaire life to small-town life in a matter of minutes, but he seemed to do it with ease. He had settled in with relatively little complaining, as far as I could see, and that fact was incredibly endearing to me.

"So, what's going to happen is, once the main area is set up and all the mechanical units are functioning properly, we're going to fill the side fields with solar panels," he said. "In fact, this whole facility, while producing green energy, will also run off green energy. It makes the carbon footprint of having it here very low. There isn't a ton of maintenance to be done unless something breaks, so the staff will be needed but nothing like a power plant and definitely not as dangerous when it comes to working conditions."

Just then, the office phone rang, but he didn't seem interested in picking it up. He turned and looked at a huge map of the property behind him, pointing out the intended solar fields. I was distracted by the phone, though.

"You should probably take the call." I chuckled.

"It's all right. I don't have to," he said.

"But you're at work." I laughed. "And surely, empires like yours were not built by ignoring phone calls."

"Maybe you're right," he said. "But I hate taking phone calls. Call me a rich snob, but I miss having a secretary to screen my calls."

"I miss having one too." I sighed. "Oh, wait. I never had a secretary."

"That's cute," he said, reaching down and grabbing the phone. "Very cute. Double R Energy Ranch. This is Lucas Henry speaking. How can I help you? ... Jeff, how are you? I almost forgot I had an appointment today. There's been a lot going on here. Could you hold on for a second? Thanks."

He put the line on hold and looked over at me smiling. That charming smile kicked me right in the gut every single time. I was pretty sure he could have told me it was the Pope, and I wouldn't have batted an eye.

"It's a journalist," he said. "The call might take a minute. I can ask them to call me back for the interview."

"Nah," I said, shaking my head and sitting down in one of the chairs. "I would love to hear an exclusive interview with a billionaire. I'm sure it'll be titillating."

He rolled his eyes and chuckled, reaching over and clicking the button, putting the call on speakerphone. He was so confident and so smooth in his motions, and it sent chills up the back of my neck. I would have been a nervous wreck to talk to a reporter, but it seemed second nature to him.

"Jeff," he said. "You still there?"

"I'm here," the reporter said.

"All right, shoot."

"How's everything going out there?" he said with a chuckle.

"It's great," Lucas said seamlessly. "We're really making some headway with everything."

I listened, impressed with his easy demeanor and instant answers to questions. I could only assume that with a project like this, they were trying to get it out to the media and show some love to the company. He had probably done dozens of interviews already.

"So, you've been pegged as a technological genius. Why this project?"

"Well, this project has been something in the making long before anyone knew my name," he said. "Green energy is the future, and not only is it good for the planet, reducing greenhouse gases, but it's just good business too. It's a way to own a responsible company, do something that means something for the people of this world, and make a living doing it."

"Now, let me ask you this," he said. "How is the project's popularity faring amongst the most recent allegations brought by Natasha Noborov and how she—?"

Before the journalist could finish the sentence, Lucas had quickly leaned forward and grabbed the handset, taking it off speakerphone. He glanced up at me, looking nervous for a moment and then leaned back in the chair, trying to play it off. I could tell something was up, though.

"My office has already commented on that subject," he said. "Thanks for taking the time to interview us here and let my PR rep know if there's anything else we can do to help. Thanks."

I was instantly intrigued, especially since he jumped to end that conversation so quickly. What allegations was the journalist talking about? And that name, Natasha someone, it sounded almost familiar in my mind. I never had a lot of time for the media, not really interested in social media, not the girl who surfed the web very often, and even television wasn't on my priority list. I had gone days, sometimes over a week, before I turned on the television, and that was usually for some noise when I was working. Alison was a different story. She was obsessed with the media. She would sit and scroll through social media for hours, reading out the latest and greatest trends going on. I, on the other hand, spent most of my time on my practice and with the horses at the charity.

Distractions were something I tried to stay away from as much as possible. There were enough things in my life that I had passion for that I didn't need to fill my time with useless crap that didn't concern me. I had been like that all my life, staying as far away from the rumor mill as possible, which was probably why I didn't have a ton of friends. Social media didn't interest me in the least, and I got enough information from Alison to satisfy any curiosity that might creep into my brain. Even social gatherings weren't really my thing, and the few friends I'd acquired when I was younger had moved away from small-town life as soon as they had the chance. It was rare to find girls like me and Alison who were happy living in the small-town Oregon landscape.

I turned my attention back to Lucas, but before I could open my mouth to ask the question about Natasha and the allegations, he was standing in front of me, grabbing my hands and pulling me to my feet. It was hard to even choke out my words when I was standing that close to him.

"I need to pay you back for coming to my rescue today." He laughed. "Why don't you come out to dinner with me at the town's only other restaurant?"

There were so many thoughts floating through my head all at once. The phone call with the journalist had my mind doing overtime, but it was hard to focus when Lucas was standing there paying me such close attention. I tried to think of what to say, but I was completely distracted when Lucas bent down and pressed his lips softly against mine. He was gentle and careful, lingering for a moment before pulling away.

"Dinner? Tonight?" I said, watching him nod his head. "Yes, of course."

I had agreed without even thinking about it. On my way home afterward, I drove along with the music playing lightly and my mind completely in the clouds. Lucas had a way of doing that to me. I glanced down up at the rearview mirror, and my heart started to pump fast and hard, seeing flashing blue lights behind me. I pulled over to the side of the road and watched in the side mirror as Gary, the deputy, pulled behind me and rolled out of the car. He pulled his belt up higher on his fat belly and walked to my window.

"Why are you pulling me over?" I asked. "I was definitely not speeding."

"You're pretty far away from home or the stables," he said, looking behind me in the van. "What are you doing all the way out in this direction?"

"I didn't know it was a crime to be out here," I growled. "I had a call about an injured animal, so I came out to take care of it. I'll be filing the report with the city like I'm supposed to."

"Right." He chuckled. "One of them city animals injured."

"Excuse me?" I said, narrowing my eyes.

"Don't play dumb," he said, looking at me with a straight face. "I know exactly where you were, and soon, Janson will too."

"What in the hell is that supposed to mean?" I asked. "What does Janson have to do with any of this?"

"Janson is only going to tolerate you pushing so far," he said, eyeing me. "Before he pushes back that is."

He tapped my window hard with his hand and nodded his head, turning and walking back to his car. I watched him climb inside and pull out, speeding away down the road toward the town. I leaned my back against the chair and breathed deeply, shaking my head. I could feel a hole in the pit of my stomach, and I knew Janson had been watching me. Everything had settled down, or at least I'd thought it had, but as soon as I thought I had a good thing going, there was Janson swooping in and fucking it up as fast as he could. This was starting to get dangerous.

Chapter 13

Lucas

I PULLED OFF MY BOOTS and set them by the door, trying not to get the dirt everywhere. After doing a few more tasks and running a couple of tests, I had come back to my room to get ready for the impromptu date I'd scheduled with Emilia. I wanted to take her out, but the date was a way for me to get her mind off the questions I knew she wanted to ask after hearing that part of the interview. I was a bit annoyed that I couldn't even take an interview in front of Emilia without the media bringing up questions about Natasha and the past. I had done several interviews with Jeff before, and he'd sideswiped me with that question, knowing full well I wasn't interested in discussing that bullshit anymore. I had panicked when I heard Natasha's name and ended the interview right then and there, which I knew wasn't going to make my PR rep very happy at all.

Hell, I had done fifty interviews about Natasha, and these new interviews were supposed to change all of that. The interviews that I agreed to were to help me move past all that bullshit, not drudge it up over and over to sell papers. I knew it was their job to ask the questions, and I had always been very patient with the media, knowing they had a huge pull on my client base and my investors' thoughts on projects, but it was getting to the point where every time I turned around, I was answering questions about that whole nightmare back in New York. I was looking forward to the day when I could take an interview and answer stupid questions like how I felt about the Mets versus the Yankees, questions that celebrities got asked during fun interviews. Instead, I got the same ones over and over again.

I changed my clothes, slinging my cell phone on the dresser and sitting down on the bed. Running my hands through my hair and groaning, it occurred to me I wasn't going to get out of this without answering to Emilia and that was the last thing I wanted to have to do. Natasha was my ex, the one I had told Emilia about the night she'd opened up about the sheriff. The thing was, I had barely scratched the surface of that whole giant disaster. Most of the time, I tried to not even think about it, much less talk about it. What had happened kept me awake for weeks, and it definitely kept my PR rep busy trying to field all of the questions and try to get some kind of good press going for me. It had been a disaster in the making from the first moment I'd laid eyes on Natasha. She was the spoiled little rich girl I'd described to Emilia, but even worse, she was devious and had her own agendas hidden behind sexy smiles and a whole lot of seduction.

Alec had warned me about her from the beginning before I'd even approached her. He'd told me she was bad news, that she was looking for more than what she was letting on. I was stupid, though, blinded by her seductive ways, that mouth, the way she seemed to be able to talk anyone into just about anything with a blink of her eyes. The thing was, though, no matter how deceitful and devious Natasha was, her father was ten times worse. She'd learned her ways from him, and when Alec was busy warning me about her, he should have been warning me about her father. I kicked myself in the ass every day for getting so caught up in that world. I was rich, yes, but they were much richer and involved in a lifestyle I had never experienced before. It was hypnotizing and drew you in deep before you even realized you were drowning.

Peter Noborov was her father's name, a rich Russian ex-pat whose business dealings ran deep in New York City. He poured his money into real estate development, sometimes winning and sometimes losing. I hadn't yet realized that was just on the surface of it all. In the end, Noborov always won, no matter what the cost. I look back at that time and almost cringe for being so stupid, so blind to what was going on around me. I thought I'd had it all figured out and didn't heed a bit of Alec's or anyone else's warnings. I'd almost completely ruined everything I had worked so hard for.

Peter doted on his daughter, thought of her as the most important piece of his life. He had no sons, and he wanted to make sure his money went somewhere safe. He had big plans for her, plans he had put into motion even before she was born. She was to marry into one of the storied American dynasties, giving her the old-world money and him the sovereignty of an American bloodline. Like everything else in Peter's life, no matter how much he loved her, she was a pawn in a bigger game. I was a new billionaire, new money, and neither he nor the rich society looked kindly upon that. I never realized there were tiers to the rich man's club until I was standing at the door trying to get in. I was the lowest of the low to them, not much above the peasants from which they made their fortunes. Peter saw Natasha with me and looked at it as her slumming, despite the billions I had in the bank. It would never have been enough for him, and nothing I could do or say would have ever changed his mind.

I didn't care about that, though. I had the hot Russian chick with the legs that went on for days and an accent that drove me wild. It was like being in some movie where the new guy got the girl, only I had forgotten to think about how those movies ended with the good guy getting the bullet too. I just wanted to have a good time, though, and at first, I knew Natasha was dating me to piss off her dad. I didn't give a shit. I was getting laid, going to the hottest parties, and men wanted to be me for the first time in my life. I got caught up in it like I had always told myself I wouldn't. But, before long, I realized things were starting to change. Natasha was getting needy, wanting more, pushing me to be around her all the time, talking about a future I had never even given two thoughts. I knew Natasha wasn't the girl for me, but she didn't seem to understand that in the least. She had her eye set on higher things, and she knew exactly what she wanted. She wanted me for life.

She wanted the forever fairy tale she thought she deserved to have, the American man giving into every single one of her desires, taking care of her, making her his wife. She wanted the fancy house, the cars, the clothes, and eventually the children to boot. She wanted to secure herself a future on her own terms, not her fathers, and she had picked me to do it with, figuring the new guy in the rich world wouldn't think two ways about it. That wasn't true, though. Beneath the haze of vodka and money that I had been traveling through since meeting her, I still was the same guy with the same dreams. I didn't want to settle down or at least not with Natasha. Playing house when she stayed with me was one thing, but truly committing to a life tied to the Nabokovs and with a girl I didn't love in the least was not in the cards for me. Even beyond the aversion to being tied down was the fact that Natasha did nothing for me beyond the sex and the booze.

I had plans to break it off with her, especially when she started talking about getting engaged, buying a place together, and moving in permanently to the penthouse. Before I could, though, everything had come crashing down like a ton of bricks. The media broke a story about Peter's involvement with the Russian oligarchy, and the words dirty money were splashed over every paper in the city. The man had used his real estate as a cover, which anyone not drowned in Natasha's charms would have seen right off the bat, but I fucked up, and I was in too deep.

As soon as the story broke, my phone began ringing off the hook, and I was getting calls from everyone including my investors and my PR team. My business reputation was in danger of guilt by association, and I knew what I had to do. I remember that day so clearly, grabbing Natasha out of the bed and taking her into the living room, sitting her down, and showing her the headlines. I had to break it off with her. There was no question. It was either going to be her or my company, and I knew without a doubt which one I wanted more. She was pissed, hurt, and very angry when I told her it was over. There was a lot of screaming, a lot of Russian, and whole lot of threats on her side. She wasn't going to take this lying down. She got everything she wanted in life, and if she didn't, she made damn sure that whoever was working against her got the shit end of the stick. She had stormed out of the penthouse that morning, and I'd thought that would be it. She would be pissed and never talk to me again, maybe keep me from going to certain clubs, but I couldn't have been more wrong.

She went straight to the papers, alleging that I was involved in several investments with her father. I had never been involved in his investments, not even for a second. Hell, I couldn't even sit in the same room with the man without him cussing at me in Russian and telling me I would never have his daughter. On top of that, she continued alleging that I knew where the money was coming from, that I willingly let that kind of illegal, treasonous activity happen and didn't say a word about it. It was ridiculous in every way, but the media lapped it up, spreading the word faster than I could dial my PR rep's phone number. I had already been the guy no one wanted to talk to in high society since my money was new, but this whole thing drove me even further out of that circle. I didn't really care about those people on a personal level, but on a business level, their support had been paramount to the future success of my company. They were the investors, the brokers, the money line to the future. That was where it all came from, and they were looking at me like a pariah.

Luckily, I had one of the best PR companies in the world on my side, and they went to work, building a team to help me out. Of course, there were questions from the feds, and I complied with everything, handing over all my paperwork and telling them everything I knew, which wasn't much. It didn't take long for them to see I had no connection other than to be the poor sap who'd dated his daughter. After that, the reputation-rebuilding PR tour commenced, and I hadn't done that many interviews in such a short amount of time, and I was pretty sure no one ever had.

I sighed and got up off the bed, pulling my shoes on and heading out to the car. My frustration over the whole situation was at its peak, but there was nothing I could do about it at that point. However, I found that the closer I got to Emilia, the more that frustration began to melt away, dropping off and awarding me some deep breaths of air. I hated how it felt to be in the center of that bullshit. It was suffocating. I was going to see Emilia again, though, and that was all that mattered to me in that moment. It wasn't like my pull to Natasha that had been completely on the surface. Emilia made me calmer, made me feel like everything was going to be okay, like there were still good people out there in the world. I knew I shouldn't keep seeing her, that it was going to suck when I left in a week, but I couldn't help myself.

When I pulled up, she was standing outside waiting for me, looking more beautiful than ever. She climbed into the car and smiled casually. On the way to the restaurant, I noticed she was a bit stiff, so I tried to lighten things by talking to her about her day. She answered shortly and kept her eyes forward on the road. Something was up, but I didn't know what it was. We went to a barbecue restaurant that night, and the food was great, but Emilia was still almost silent the whole time. I tried again to lighten the mood, telling her a story about the only barbeque Alec had hosted at his mansion in the Hamptons. Alec had spent thousands on the perfect barbecue setup only to discover it was a bit harder than it looked on television.

"He burned every piece of meat he tried to cook." I laughed.

Finally, a smile broke through, and Emilia began to laugh, making me feel a hell of a lot better. The mood had lightened, and I could enjoy my time with her again. She had become paramount in my life here in Bonanza, and I wasn't sure what I would do when it was over.

Chapter 14

Emilia

I COULD SEE THIS ALEC guy, all suited up in a thousand-dollar dress shirt and an apron that said "Kiss the Chef" on the front of it, his grill practically on fire. I couldn't help but laugh. It was definitely the most awkward thing I could imagine happening in a place like the Hamptons, which I had only heard of in magazines and movies. I took a bite of my food and shook my head, looking up at Lucas.

"Have you ever done any of your own cooking?" I asked. "Or do you have an army of butlers cater everything for you?"

Lucas threw his head back and laughed, a real, deep, genuine laugh. It was almost contagious, and I found myself giggling at him. He was so cute with those dimples and that perfect smile. It was almost hard to believe he was a real person sitting across from me.

"No butlers." He laughed, taking a drink of his beer. "Not even a cook. I've been feeding myself since I was old enough to use a stove, which was probably still too young by normal family standards. My mother worked two jobs, one that started at about eleven in the morning working for a dry cleaner down the street and the other an overnight shift at the diner. She barely ever slept, and when she was home, she was either taking a quick nap before the next shift or tending to some mess my father had made. I was put in charge of cooking dinner for the family, even if the words weren't actually spoken. It was that or my mother didn't eat, and I lived off cereal and whatever I could scrounge out of the fridge."

"Wow," I said. "My mom taught me to cook but not until I was older."

"I have to say," he said, smiling. "Even though I do all the cooking for myself, it's nice to know that if I wanted to, I could pay someone else to do the hard work and cleanup, especially the cleanup. I hate doing the dishes and even more so when I'm only cooking for myself. It took me a while to learn how to cook for one person. My first six months of living alone, my fridge was constantly full of leftovers because I cooked enough for an army."

"I know how that feels. I used to do the same thing." I smiled. "As far as affording someone to clean up and do the hard work, I would imagine it would feel good to be able to afford to do that, especially after working your way up from where you came from. It's nice to see that you haven't forgotten where you came from. That's important to remember. Still, I'd really like to see you cook sometime, find out what that rich boy palette is really like."

"You mean like sloppy joes?" He laughed.

"Oh, no." I smiled and then giggled. "Why does that not surprise me?"

"Hey, I have an idea," he said, his eyes heating up as he looked over at me. "Why don't you let me cook you a poor boy, rich boy breakfast tomorrow morning. You can see what I can do first thing in the morning, you get fed, and I get an excuse to spend more time with you. As you can see, I've been looking for any excuse to spend more time with you, even getting barbecue sauce all over my face and telling you horror stories from my childhood."

I shifted in my seat, putting my hands in my lap and gripping my napkin tightly. I knew exactly what he was trying to say, and it wasn't for him to come over first thing in the morning but instead for him to still be there from the night before. I could already imagine us sitting around the breakfast table, feeding our stomachs after a hot night in the bedroom. Just thinking about it made me weak in the knees, and I could feel the heat almost radiating off my skin. What was so wrong about that anyway? We were two adults, two consenting adults, who were having a blast being around each other. The sexual tension between us was growing stronger by the minute, and we had obviously been attracted to each other since the first time we'd met. Maybe it was time I invited him over and saw exactly what he could do with that bulge I felt pressing against my side that night in my kitchen.

Then, my mind shifted, and I remembered Janson and the fact that he and his cronies were keeping a really tight watch on me. He had already sent his deputy after me, watching me as I went out to the ranch, and there was a serious possibility he had something to do with the animals in my driveway. Who knew what he would do if he found out Lucas had stayed over at my place? He was a wild card, one I wasn't particularly interested in playing with. It would be like playing with fire, only I knew exactly who would get burned, and neither Lucas or I needed that in our lives. Janson was not someone to be fooled with.

I could feel Lucas staring at me intently across the table, and as much as I wanted to invite him over, I knew I couldn't. I needed to change the subject, to get our minds on something else so I could avoid the discomfort of the moment. I didn't want him to think I wasn't interested, but at the same time, I didn't want to tell him about Janson and how he'd been basically stalking me since Lucas and I started seeing each other.

"So," I said, clearing my throat. "Do you do a lot of interviews like the one you did today?"

"Yeah," he said with a smirk, watching me divert the attention. "I definitely do my fair share. There was a lot of attention when I sold that system to the social media site, and then it kind of escalated from there. It can be a good thing and a bad thing, but that's why I have a PR team to schedule all of that, talk about what questions I won't be answering, and try to push the interviews in a positive manner. I'm pretty open to them, though. It helps with business."

"That sounds absolutely miserable." I laughed. "Having to expose my personal life to everyone in the world. Having people scrutinize everything about my life from what I was wearing to what decisions I made. I don't think I could handle living like that. I don't know how you do it, and I especially don't know how people like movie stars and musicians do it, either, people who are constantly in the public eye. I like my little, private, boring life with the only person asking me what I'm doing is the horse in the stables during feeding time."

"Do you hear horses, sweetie?" He chuckled. "If you hear horses, we should go talk to someone and not a journalist."

"No." I laughed, throwing my napkin at him. "I'm an introvert. I like my me time, and I like only choosing to talk to certain people. I don't understand how people can do it constantly being in the public eye like that. Everyone's always watching, judging, making assumptions that aren't true. It would drive me absolutely crazy, and on top of that, I have thin skin. I would be hunting down reporters left and right who lied about me and my life like in tabloids."

"I understand that, and trust me, it's not something I enjoy in the least," he said. "When I started all of this, I never even thought about that side of the coin, about the public's intervention into my private life, but when it came, I had to learn to accept it. I didn't realize how important the PR part of a company really is. It can literally make you or break you. It's a way to monitor my brand and try to maneuver the news in a way that keeps the public's perception of me and the company positive."

He made a lot of sense, but I still felt bad that he had to deal with it like that. When dinner was done, I felt that regretful feeling again, not wanting the evening to end. I could see in Lucas's eyes that he felt the exact same way, but I knew I couldn't invite him back to my house. He put his napkin on his plate and smiled at me.

"You know what?"

"What?" I smiled.

"I'm not ready for the night to end. Let's go for a drive," he said.

"I like that idea," I replied.

We headed out of town, driving under the twinkling stars. I directed him to a butte with a nice lookout that I figured we could stargaze under. We pulled out past the trees and got out of the car. I stretched my arms up over my head and walked over beside Lucas, looking down at the beautiful town lights sparkling beneath us. It was one of my favorite places in town. He put his arm around me and kept me close to him.

"I had a really nice time in your little town," he whispered. "And it's all because of you."

I turned and looked into his eyes, breathless from his words. He leaned down and pressed his lips against mine, kissing me gently. I reached up and wrapped my arms around his neck, feeling the passion ignite between us. It was suddenly my new favorite place to be.

Chapter 15

Lucas

MY LIPS WERE PRESSED hard against Emilia's, and I couldn't believe how addictive her taste was. She was the most enchanting creature I had ever had in my arms, and I was struggling to control myself. I picked her up around the waist and turned, leaning her back against the SUV, trailing my lips down her neck and over her collarbone. She gasped lightly, goosebumps forming all over where my lips touched. She grasped tightly to my shirt, spreading her legs apart and wrapping them around me. I ran my hand up her side and brought my face back to hers, pressing my mouth to hers. I ran my tongue over her lips, and she opened up, taking me inside. I groaned, tasting the passion of her lips, wanting more and more of her. Things were so hot and so heavy, and I stepped back as she pulled away, sliding down onto her feet. She gripped onto the hood of the truck, finding herself as weak in the knees as I was.

"We have to slow down," she said, breathing heavily.

"I understand." I stepped forward and kissed her forehead. "Come on. I'll take you home."

I drove her home and got out of the car, walking her up to the front door. I cupped her cheeks in my hands and kissed her passionately one last time before pulling back and looking deeply into her eyes. She turned toward the door, smiling, but I dropped my hands to hers and turned her back around.

"I know this is probably crazy and very sudden, but I can't get my mind off you, not even for a moment," I said. "Come away with me tomorrow, just the two of us."

"Where?" She giggled.

"I won a night at a winery bed and breakfast at the auction," I said.

"Oh, the one you paid ten times the current bid for?" She laughed. "I only got five times the current bid."

"Too little in my mind," I smiled. "But I want to spend that vacation with you. Originally, I was going to give it away to someone in town, thinking a solo trip to a winery would be depressing in some ways. But now, I have someone I want to be with there. It would be an amazing way to end my time here, just being with the person who made it so special."

Emilia's skin was flushed, and her eyes twinkled in the moonlight. She shifted in her stance and looked down at her hands. I could tell she was torn. She wanted to come, but there was something holding her back from giving in. I didn't want to pressure her, to make her feel like it was necessary that she say yes. Everything between the two of us had been a whirlwind, and she knew I was going to be leaving very soon. I smiled and tilted her chin up to me, leaning forward and kissing her gently once again. Her lips were so soft and so perfect, and it was incredibly hard to pull away from her.

"How about this," I said with a smile. "Take some time to think about it. I don't want to pressure you, and I won't be upset if you say no. Call me in the morning with your answer."

"All right," she said with a shy smile. "Thank you for dinner. It was really lovely."

"Anytime." I smiled. "You go inside, get snuggled in, and have amazing dreams tonight."

She nodded and turned, walking into the house. When I knew she was securely locked away, I turned and went back to my car, feeling like I was on cloud nine all over again. I got in my car and sat there for a moment, thinking about her lips and the possibility of having her all to myself for at least one night. I put the car in drive and headed back toward the hotel. As I drove along the dark strip, something caught my eye. I looked in my rearview mirror and saw flashing blue lights behind me. Instantly, I gripped the steering wheel, unsure of what to expect. I drove a little farther to where there was a streetlight and pulled the car over on the side of the road. The police car pulled up behind me, and I watched in my side mirror as the sheriff got out and started walking toward my SUV. He had one hand on his pistol, and his hat was shadowing his face.

Sheriff Janson walked up to my window that I had rolled down and looked at me with dark eyes. I breathed deeply, both of my hands on the steering wheel. I hadn't been speeding or anything like that, so I knew this visit was more than just routine. He had followed me. I could tell it by the look in his eyes.

"Evening," he growled. "Please step out of the vehicle."

Immediately, I was on edge, wanting to protest but knowing in a small town like that, it really wouldn't do me any good. There was no one to complain to, and it was obvious Janson did anything but follow the law in that town. He was more a bully than a sheriff. I sighed and reluctantly got out of the car, keeping my hands where he could see them. I didn't want to give him any excuse to pull out his gun.

"It's pretty late out," he said, lifting the front of his cowboy hat and looking me in the face. "Where you coming from?"

I stood there looking at him, debating on what to answer him with. I wanted to assert my dominance and tell him the truth, really driving it home, but I knew that was probably a bad idea. The whole situation was a bad idea, so I went with the safe approach.

"I was dropping a friend of mine off at home," I said.

"That's interesting." He chuckled.

"Why is that?" I replied, still staring directly into his eyes.

"I just think it's strange seeing you've only been in town for a few days, maybe a week," he said. "You must be one hell of a guy, making friends really fast."

"I like to think I'm a friendly guy," I said back. "I tend to attract like-minded people."

"I really doubt there are any like-minded people in this town," he said. "We don't tend to keep the same views as rich boys from the big city. In fact, we don't tend to take too kindly to people like you."

"You'd be surprised how much in common I have with these folks," I said, standing up straight.

"I think I'd be surprised if you had anything in common with the shit that falls out of the cow's ass in the field." He smirked. "How many friends you planning on taking back and forth while you're here?"

"I guess that depends on how many friends I make, now doesn't it?"

"I think you should be more focused on getting the hell out of town than making friends," he said.

"Why is that?"

"Well, I grew up here, my daddy grew up here, his daddy before that, and so on," he said. "This town has always done things a certain way, and if it ain't broke, then it don't need fixin.'"

"Oh, I don't know about that." I smiled. "I think change can do good for most places."

"I think I don't like people like you, loose morals, thinking you can flash your money around and have whatever you want, coming into my town," he said. "And even worse than that, trying to change the town and how certain people feel."

The tension between the two of us was extremely thick. I could almost smell the liquor on Janson's breath as he breathed heavily in front of me. He had a real complex, thinking he could tell people what to do and how to think. The worst part about it was, I knew he was trying to warn me away from Emilia, and it pissed me off to no end. He was a controller, someone who would do anything and say anything to keep control of as much as he could. He looked at Emilia like the dairy farm looked at their cows, nothing more than property to control. I had upset that for him, and now he was trying to bully me.

"I don't think you understand what I'm saying," Janson said, taking a step forward.

"Oh, I completely understand," I said, watching him move even closer.

I couldn't handle him in my space like that, so I reached up and pushed him as hard as I could, watching him stumble back. I moved quickly, raising my arm to slug him, but then I stopped, looking down to his side at his hand on the butt of his gun. He smirked over at me, tapping his fingers against his pistol. I knew it was no use, so I put my hand down and held my tongue, completely enraged by this douchebag standing in front of me. He pulled his jacket straight and cleared his throat, spitting to the side.

"I'll tell you what I'm gonna do," he said. "I'm in a good mood tonight, so I'm going to let you off with a warning. I think you know what that warning is. Next time, though, I can promise you, I won't go so easy on your ass."

I stood there, breathing heavily, every muscle in my body tense as hell. I watched as he laughed, walking back to his car and climbing inside. He turned off the bright flashing lights and pulled out, slowing down and tipping his hat as he passed. Had I been any more tired, been the least bit intoxicated, or been any younger, I would have beat the hell out of the man, probably getting shot in the process. I growled, turning around and getting into my car, pounding my fists on the steering wheel. When I had calmed a bit, I headed back to the hotel, not saying a word as I passed the front desk and headed back to my room. I sat on the edge of the bed, pulling off my clothes, feeling totally enraged and almost out of control with everything.

Throughout the night, I tossed and turned in bed, having nightmares like I had never experienced before. Janson was there threatening Emilia, and I was literally glued to the spot I was in. I was completely helpless to intervene, watching the whole thing go down right in front of my eyes. I had never felt like that before, so angry, so protective of a woman like that. When I woke up the next morning, I was in a terrible mood, still feeling the sting of confrontation between me and the sheriff. I wanted to give him a piece of mind, really let him know how small he was, but before I could, my phone rang, and it was Emilia.

"Hey," I said. "Good to hear your voice."

"I want to go to the bed and breakfast with you," she blurted out excitedly. "I knew as soon as you left, so I took the night, and I packed all of my stuff. I want to go tonight if that's okay."

"That sounds fantastic," I said, my mood lightening almost instantly. "I'm gonna pack, and I'll come get you."

"All right," she said happily.

I jumped out of bed feeling almost like a new man. I grabbed a bag and packed my things, hurrying so I could pick her up as soon as possible. I wanted to get both of us out of that town, even if was just for the night. I needed to be alone with Emilia, and I didn't want Janson anywhere close.

Chapter 16

Emilia

AFTER LUCAS HAD LEFT the night before, I sat alone in the kitchen sipping a cup of tea. I knew in the back of my mind that I wanted to go with him. I just had to get there. The next morning after getting off the phone with him, I stood in the hallway packed and ready to go, excited about the decision I was making. I woke up early that morning and rescheduled all my Monday appointments knowing we wouldn't be back in time. I was really looking forward to an extra day off, something I never did. Even when the practice was closed, I was usually slaving away in the stables taking care of the horses and helping Alison with whatever maintenance needed to take place. This was going to be two full days of doing whatever I wanted to do, and I didn't have to answer one phone call or go on any house calls during that time.

I was pretty sure the last time I took a weekday off from work was when my parents were moving, and I helped drive them up to Phoenix and then came straight back. Even that wasn't really a vacation, so this one was extra special. I might even go wild and have a little too much to drink that night, knowing I wouldn't have to wake up early for anyone, and I also would be right there at the winery. I had never gotten to go to a winery before, and the idea of it seemed fancy and luxurious to me. I knew Lucas felt differently about it, but he wasn't going for the luxury. He was going for me. He wanted to be alone with me, spend some time, just the two of us without worrying about work, other people, or what people might say about it.

Janson was going to figure I was home since my car would stay parked out front, and unless he was still following me, there was a really good chance he wouldn't find out about it. The winery was in the next county over, a place where he had no jurisdiction and didn't have the kind of manpower in Bonanza to send someone to find me. I didn't care at that moment, anyway. I was too excited about getting away with Lucas and really getting to know him better. Just at that thought, I looked out the window and saw Lucas pulling into the driveway. He got out of the car and smiled as I opened the front door. He walked straight up to me and took me in his arms, hugging me excitedly.

"You ready to get out of here for a while?"

"You don't even know how ready I am." I laughed.

"Let's get your bags." He smiled, reaching down and picking up my suitcase.

I grabbed my bookbag, slinging it over my shoulder and locking the door behind me. I looked around quickly but saw no sign of anyone around. I tossed my bag in the backseat and smiled as Lucas opened the door for me. We hit the road, the radio on and the windows cracked. I could already tell it was going to be an amazing day. I smiled, riding out of the city and into the open country. It was one of the most beautiful days it had been in a long time, with bright sun shining down on us and not a cloud in the sky. It was like the weather was reflecting my feelings, and I didn't know how it could get much better than this. Then, Lucas reached down and took my hand, looking over at me and smiling.

"I'm really glad you agreed to come away with me," he said.

I smiled at him, showing him how happy I was that I decided to come away too. For a moment, it looked like I'd knocked him off-kilter, like he didn't know how to respond. He looked almost lost, staring into my eyes, watching me in the sunshine. He made me feel that way, too, so many times, but it was the first time I'd caught that look on his face. A look like I was the only girl in the world, and he had just figured it out, right there in the middle of the highway on a beautiful sunny day. I laughed and turned, looking out at the road ahead of us. Butterflies blew through my stomach, and I glanced back over him, watching him smile to himself as he drove. I loved that I had that effect on him, that he couldn't keep his feelings off his face anymore. I had never had that kind of effect on a man before, and I didn't think I ever would.

I had seen that look before, though, when I used to watch my mom sitting at the table and my father walk up behind her with flowers he picked from the field. She would smile, closing her eyes and sniffing the flowers. My father would have that same exact look on his face like he had realized all over again how special she was to him.

I looked around me and realized I was familiar with where we were. Bonanza was on one side of the county, and we had to drive all the way through to get to the next one where the winery was. My parents used to take me to this little, hidden beach to swim when I was a kid. I smiled and bit my lip, wondering if he would be up for a little adventure on our way to the bed and breakfast. I looked over and patted his leg.

"You up for a little detour?"

"Hell, yeah," he said, smiling.

"Take the next exit and turn right." I smiled.

When we got off the exit, we drove slowly through a little town, looking around at all the people coming out of church and heading to the same ice cream parlor my parents would take me to after a day of swimming. I led him down a dirt road that ended at a shallow river beach. It was vacant and beautiful with the water splashing up on the shore and the birds flying high overhead. Lucas got out of the car and smiled over at me, looking around at the beautiful landscape. It was the perfect place to stretch our legs, and I wished I had thought of packing a lunch for a picnic. It was a little early for lunch anyway. It was a relatively warm day, just coming out of the break of the frost on that side of Oregon. He took my hand and led me down the small embankment onto the sand. I sat down and took off my shoes and socks and rolled up my pant legs. Lucas was on the same page and reached down to help me up. We walked out into the water, wading in up to our calves and feeling the cold river water rush over our feet. I laughed loudly, watching Lucas waver, almost falling over as he stepped on a rock. I closed my eyes and looked up toward the sun, feeling the beauty of the day wash over my entire body.

Suddenly, water sprayed over my face, and I smiled, slowly opening my eyes and looking over at him. He had a playful grin on his face, and his hand was dripping water. We both moved at the same time, splashing water in each other's direction. I screamed out laughing, running from him as he swiped his hand through the water in my direction. He took off after me, grabbing me around the waist from behind and bending me toward the water. I laughed out, begging for him not to do it.

"I'll do it," he said, laughing. "I'll dip you right over into that cold water."

"I'll take you right along with me," I yelled out between laughs.

"Is that right?" He laughed, struggling to bend and then picking me up, cradling me in his arms. "I think I might have the upper hand here."

"I don't think so," I said, wrapping my arms around his neck and holding on for dear life. "If I'm going in, you're going to have one hell of a fight on your hands. You don't know how hard I can hold onto someone. You'll topple right over headfirst into the water."

"Maybe you're right," he said, pretending to let go and smiling at my scream.

He turned and walked back toward the shore, laughing loudly as he carried me. I still clung to his neck tightly, not trusting him until I saw sand beneath us. Slowly, I uncrossed my arms and leaned back, looking deeply into his eyes. Both of our smiles faded into passion, and I leaned forward, pressing my lips to his. I could taste the water on his lips, and he breathed heavily into my mouth, both out of breath from the swim and out of breath from the lust bubbling up between us. He dropped to his knees and laid me down on the beach, leaning over me and kissing me passionately. I moved my hands through his hair as he swirled his tongue around my mouth, tasting me, having me. Between the fresh air, the excitement, and the attraction between us, I was beside myself.

He leaned into me, kissing me harder, making out with me like we were teenagers hiding from our parents.

The thrill of it was invigorating, and I could feel the heat of need simmering deep down in my stomach. He ran his hand up under my shirt and grabbed my breast, pushing a light moan from my throat. The sound aroused him further, and he groaned, kissing me feverishly. He pulled his hand back out and just as he was about to go for the button on my jeans, another car pulled up. He pulled back and looked into my eyes with a smile.

"They're here to get you," I laughed, pulling myself up and helping him to his feet.

He took my hand, and we ran toward the SUV, laughing loudly like children. He nodded at the family getting out of the car next to us and opened my door, giving me his hand and bowing as I climbed inside. I giggled, watching him close the door and almost skip around to the driver's side.

"I say we grab an ice cream cone and head out toward the winery," he said.

"That sounds like a perfect idea."

We pulled out of the drive and down the dirt road, listening to the music and dancing around. Suddenly, I wished there weren't so many miles left to the winery. I was on fire for Lucas. I could feel it all over my body. I couldn't wait to get him alone, to let him take me in our little hideaway vacation spot. I breathed deeply trying to get myself under control, but from the look of the bulge in Lucas's pants, he was struggling through the same thing.

We grabbed an ice cream cone and headed out toward the winery, covered in sand and water. It was the best day I'd ever had with a man, and I knew it would always be part of my memories after he was gone. I didn't want to think about that, though. I wanted to think about that passionate kiss and how every turn of the wheel brought me closer to ecstasy.

Chapter 17

Lucas

I HAD TO ADMIT, NO matter how fun that drive was, no matter how much I enjoyed the sunshine shining down through the windows, I was really glad when we finally arrived at the winery. It had been the point of the whole trip, but the drive there made me know that being with Emilia was what I wanted. After the swim in the river on the drive over, I felt like I was being tortured. Every move Emilia made turned me on, and I couldn't help moving my eyes over every part of her body whenever she was looking the opposite way. I was pretty sure I had been caught a couple of times, but I didn't care, I wasn't trying to hide the fact that I wanted her. I was pretty sure that had been understood since the first night I'd talked to her, even more so when we'd kissed for the first time.

As soon as I'd put my lips to Emilia's at the beach, my cock started to struggle. It had been an upward battle every moment after that. The only time I had been able to keep my mind off it was in the ice cream shop and that was from all the people around us. Even in the car, watching her lick that cone was agony. My cock had been throbbing ever since then, which made the ride eternally long and eternally hard to pay full attention to. I did my best, though, trying to calm myself down by focusing on the road. That proved harder than I thought as well, and I found myself swerving the steering wheel several times to avoid running off the road. It was hell trying to keep my eyes on the road because they kept sneaking back over to her sitting in the passenger seat. Her shirt had been wet for half of the trip, and her heaving breasts and hard nipples were more than a distraction. They were a visual torture hell-bent on running me right off into a ditch. At least then, I would have been sitting still.

The last half hour of the trip, I had kept my hand on her thigh, squeezing it every so often and smiling over at her. I could see the lust and desire in her eyes, and I knew she was thinking the same thing as me. We both wanted to get to the bed and breakfast and just rip into each other, but we had to be patient, something I had always been pretty good at until that moment in the car. I had to keep telling myself not to slide my hand up farther, to keep right where it was. When we saw the sign for the winery, I was pretty sure I could have jumped for joy.

We turned down the dirt road and drove slowly through rows and rows of grapes, starting to sprout in the warming sunshine. Emilia looked excitedly out the window, and I realized she had probably never been to a winery before. The thought had never even crossed my mind, especially since I had been to my fair share, especially when I'd traveled to California and overseas for work. After about five minutes, we finally made it to the main house. I parked the car in the small lot in front of the house and looked over at Emilia with a big grin. She leaned over and kissed my cheek tenderly, giving me a knowing look.

I got out of the car and chuckled, watching her walk out into the sunshine and look over the hills of grapes growing in the distance. I opened the car and grabbed our bags, throwing her backpack over my shoulder. She looked over at me and smiled, hurrying to catch up. We walked inside to the counter, and I set the bags on the floor and glanced around me. I was impressed with the rustic grace of the house and was starting to think this would be even better than I thought.

"Hello," a woman's voice rang out, coming from the back.

The woman was middle-aged with long brown hair tied at the nape of her neck. She had the kind of clothes rich housewives would wear from tiny boutiques they went into when vacationing in the mountains. No labels, mostly handmade, but her accent jewelry showed she was a little whimsical. I was very familiar with this kind of woman. She was obviously bored, her husband always gone on business, her children or child grown and in college. So, she bought a bed and breakfast not far away, and it was the horny customers who were currently keeping her entertained for the moment. She probably had a full staff to run the winery and then took her time meticulously picking out every stitch of furniture, every picture, and every bedspread, finding satisfaction in her "uncanny" ability to turn an old farmhouse into a chalet for those wanting to get out of town.

"Hi." I smiled. "Lucas and Emilia, here for the night."

"Yes, yes." She smiled. "You're the winning bidders for the gift certificate from Bonanza."

"Yes, ma'am," I said.

"Wonderful. Let me show you to your room." She smiled.

I picked up the bags and walked behind Emilia who was trying to keep up with the woman. She looked back at me and held in a giggle, almost running into the innkeeper as she stopped to talk about a painting on the wall. This went on the entire way up three flights of stairs, and my arms were burning by the time we reached the top. Luckily, the hallway was short up there because staring at Emilia's ass was getting me hard all over again. In fact, the whole tour was complete and total agony. All I wanted to do was get to the room, put down the bags, throw Emilia on the bed, and spend the next several hours making love to her. I had been tortured on the entire drive and, now, all the way up to the room. It was like karma was sitting on my shoulder having a ball watching me struggle through the long wait. I didn't think I had ever wanted someone as much as I wanted her right then.

The innkeeper stopped one last time and showed us some bench that was circa—hell, I don't know. I stopped listening. Finally, she reached the door and opened it with an old skeleton key. She showed us inside and pointed out the different amenities to Emilia as I lugged the suitcases in and dropped them on the floor. I leaned back against the dresser and panted, feeling like my heart was beating out of my chest.

Maybe I wasn't in as good of shape as I originally thought. Now, all I had to do was wait out the last few minutes of the woman standing there, telling us about the wine tour and where to find her if we needed anything. I felt almost triumphant as she handed Emilia the key and smiled sweetly. I stood up, gripping my fists together in anticipation as she walked toward the door. She stopped and turned around, forcing me to act nonchalant.

"Dinner is included in your stay," she said. "It will be served on the terrace in less than an hour."

She smiled and turned around, walking from the room and closing the door behind her. I put my arms up in the air with my mouth wide and groaned loudly, dropping them to my side and hanging my head. Of course, my cock took over and the scheming and debating began. Did I say screw it and knock one out of the park real fast? Did I take a cold shower and just deal with it? I looked over at Emilia who was bent over, looking in her suitcase. I quickly shut my eyes and breathed in through my nose and out through my mouth, just like I was taught to do when I was anxious. A lot could be done in an hour, that was for damn sure, but at the same time, I didn't want to rush it. I didn't want to have to stop so we didn't go hungry for the night. The innkeeper also seemed like the kind of woman who would come looking for us if we didn't show up for dinner. It was probably for the best since I didn't want to rush things. She deserved to be paid attention to, to have me fawn all over her body.

I adjusted my pants and turned toward Emilia, smiling as she looked up at me holding a small black dress. I could already imagine her in the thing, and it was starting to make my head dizzy. She looked at me confused, and I forced a smile on my face.

"How about this for dinner?" she asked.

"Looks good," I said.

I knew one thing for sure. I couldn't stay in that room with her. Otherwise, I would be all over her in minutes, and this time, there would be no stopping us.

"Okay, I'll change in the bathroom, and you can change out here." She smiled, prancing past me.

"Afterward, let's go for a walk," I yelled.

"Sounds good," she said through the door.

When we both had changed and gotten all the sand off us, we headed outside to the vineyard, holding hands as we walked. The sun was getting lower in the sky, and she looked absolutely gorgeous in the light. I was almost stunned by how much I was taken back by it. We talked lightly about the trip, about the inn, and she laughed loudly, replaying my face as I struggled behind them with the suitcases. Little did she know that was only a small portion of my struggle. We headed back to the house, hearing the sound of the dinner chimes that the innkeeper rang out over the vineyard. We were the only ones there for dinner, and there was a beautiful table set with candles and a knit cloth over the table. We sat down across from each other, putting our napkins in our laps as she served our appetizers and a beautiful display of the vineyard's own wine. I was actually very impressed by it all.

Once the main course was served, the innkeeper scampered off, leaving us to have our privacy. I looked to the right over the hills and shook my head at the beauty. The sun was starting to set below the horizon, and the sky was a mix of fiery oranges and bright reds. It had to be one of the most beautiful sunsets I had ever seen, especially since I rarely saw them in the city. I reached across the table and took Emilia's hand, enjoying the quiet tranquility of the moment. The warm breeze blew across the vineyard, and I could see the bright streaks of mahogany shimmering in Emilia's hair.

I knew in that moment there was nowhere else on earth I would have chosen to be in that moment. I was right where I wanted to be, right where I was supposed to be. Emilia looked over at me and smiled, her eyes twinkling brightly. I felt like an extremely lucky man to have met her. She was like an unexpected jewel in a rough situation. She started to speak but as she did, the innkeeper came out with a cart of desserts. Emilia smiled, but I could see the lust in her eyes, and I realized she was as eager as I was.

Chapter 18

Emilia

I WAS HUNGRY. AFTER that long drive, there was no doubt about that, but my mind was somewhere completely different. It felt like dinner was taking forever, and the only time I slowed down to stop and enjoy the moment was during the sunset when I noticed Lucas looking at me like he was the luckiest man on earth. It was a beautiful moment, a beautiful place really, with the grapes cascading over the hills and the sun setting right over them like they were being swallowed whole. It was probably the most romantic moment I had ever experienced. The rest, though, was almost painful. There was course after course with appetizers, soups, salads, main courses, and finally dessert. In between that, there were even more wine samplings. The innkeeper wanted to know how we felt about every single one, not like either of us was going to say something bad. You could tell in the woman's eyes that it was her pride and joy. It was making me a bit dizzy, though, with all the booze on top of the martinis that had been served with dinner. Lucas was going to have to carry me up to the room if I wasn't careful.

During the sunset, I couldn't get Lucas's hot body off my mind, and though I was enjoying the slow, romantic feel of it, about ten minutes in, I was ready to go. I contemplated telling him how I felt, how much I wanted him, how much I enjoyed being there with him. I started to open my mouth to say that when the innkeeper walked out with a tray of desserts.

"Everything is homemade, and please, feel free to try them all," she said, sitting three plates down on the table.

"Thank you," I said, forcing a smile.

I won't lie. I rushed through dessert, and Lucas probably thought I was crazy, but I only wanted to get back to the room. I wanted him more than I had ever wanted anyone, and I had really hoped we could have gotten it out of our systems when we got back. Unfortunately, dinner was served very quickly so we didn't have time, though I was pretty sure I could have made it happen. I didn't want to rush it, though, so I'd changed, and we'd gone for a walk instead. I knew if I had stayed in that room with him, we would have had an innkeeper knocking on the door, looking for us for dinner. Lucas watched as the woman walked back inside to get something.

"This is beautiful and romantic," he said, shaking his head.

"But you want to get back to the room?"

"Holy hell, yes." He chuckled.

At that moment, the woman came back outside and gave us a bottle of dessert wine to take with us upstairs. I smiled and thanked her, looking over at Lucas. He wanted me too. There was no mistaking it, and I felt a lot better knowing I wasn't the only one struggling through the end of dinner. I also kind of liked that he was sitting there thinking about all the things he wanted to do to me when we got upstairs. It was arousing, and I couldn't wait to see it. We sat there talking casually with the innkeeper, listening to her stories about the vineyard, the house, and how she came to own the place. It was all very enthralling, but I could have cared less. When the moment came to politely excuse ourselves from the table and wish the hovering, overly-helpful woman a good night, we took it. We walked quietly back into the house and around the corner. As soon as we were out of her sight, Lucas grabbed my hand and pulled me quickly up the stairs. We were moving so fast, we were pretty much jogging at that point.

We got up to our floor and stopped for a minute, out of breath from running up three flights of stairs. I really needed to remember to start working out more when we got back home. We walked over to the door, and he pulled the key out of his pocket, fumbling with it in the knob. I giggled, taking it from him and opening the door. He walked in first, and I walked behind him, turning and closing the door behind us. As I turned around, I looked at Lucas staring at me with heat in his eyes. He moved forward quickly and shoved me up against the door, immediately starting to kiss me. I breathed deeply, feeling his hands roaming all over my body as we kissed passionately. I was so hot, I could barely stand it. I wanted to rip his clothes off and fuck the hell out of him right there on the floor. I leaned my head up and looked at the ceiling as he trailed his lips down my neck, trying to slow myself down. I was on fire, hotter and more aroused than I had ever been with anyone in my life. I could tell he felt the same way as he moved back up and looked deeply into my eyes.

I reached up and brought his head back toward mine, feeling his mouth ravaging mine. His tongue swirled through my mouth, and I could taste the bittersweet red wine on his lips from dinner. We stood there against the wall, making out for quite a while, feeling the pressure between us building at every turn. He slowed his mouth down and ran his lips across mine, barely touching them. He moved over my cheek and down my neck, listening to the breath catching in my throat. I could feel the electricity shooting through my stomach and the heat boiling between my legs. He pulled back and looked at me seductively, moving his fingers to the side of my dress and pulling down the zipper.

I bit my bottom lip and reached up, carefully unbuttoning his expensive dress shirt. I pulled it open and looked at his hard, tanned chest, running my fingers across the scars and tattoos that covered him. I'd had no idea he had ink under there, but the mixture of the two was so hot, and he went from sexy man to hot bad boy really fast in my eyes. He reached down, grabbed the bottom of my dress, and pulled it up over my head, tossing it to the side. His hands moved to my back and unclasped my bra, letting my breasts spill out into his hands. I groaned, feeling his rough skin massage my tender breasts, and immediately, I needed more. I pulled his shirt off him and unbuckled his belt, taking time to undo the button and pull down the zipper. His cock was bulging beneath his pants, and I bit my lip again as I watched them slide to his feet.

He stepped forward and cupped my hot, wet pussy, rubbing his fingers over the satin of my panties. I moaned out, reaching down and grabbing onto his cock, my eyes widening at the enormity of it. He kissed my lips softly while he slid his boxers to his ankles before reaching out to do the same with my panties. As he rose back up and kissed my thighs, he stopped for a moment and gazed up at me. He dropped down to his knees and spread my legs apart, kissing my abdomen lightly as he slid his fingers through my folds. I moaned, leaning my head back against the door and closing my eyes as he pushed through my juices and pressed two fingers up inside of me.

I reached up and grabbed my breasts, feeling him begin to move them in and out of me over and over. He reached up with his other hand and spread my lips apart, lapping softly at my clit. I gasped, feeling the pure pleasure of it all, spreading my legs wider and running my hand down through his curly, blond hair. I could feel the heat burning inside of me as he started to suck harder on my nub, fingering me with an even, steady pace. I tried to move, but he pushed me back against the door, holding me there as he licked me further toward climax. I gripped down on the back of his head as he pushed a third finger inside of me, glancing up to see me scream out in pleasure. I began to move my hips, slowly at first and then picking up the pace. I ground my clit onto his mouth, feeling his warm tongue rub circles over it. I reached my other hand up above my head and groaned, wanting to feel him inside of me.

As he picked up the pace with his fingers, I began to pant, looking down at him with an open mouth. I wanted to scream out, to say anything, but I was left breathless at the feeling. I grabbed his head with two hands and tugged upward. He kissed my clit one last time and stood up slowly, his fingers still inside of me. His face was just inches from mine, and he looked deeply into my eyes, pushing his hand up and down as the tips of his fingers fluttered wildly inside of me. I gasped and leaned forward, kissing his mouth and then pulling back.

"I want you," I panted. "I want you inside of me."

He smiled and stayed put for another moment before pulling his fingers out and reaching around me, grabbing me by the ass and lifting me up in the air. He pushed my back against the door and grabbed his cock, gliding it through my juices and pushing upward, deep inside of me. I groaned, rolling my eyes and throwing my head back, feeling his body pressing hard against mine. He thrust his hips forward, digging deep and stopping, rolling his hips against my clit. I gripped down onto his shoulders and gritted my teeth, feeling myself teetering on the edge of orgasm. He could see it in my eyes and began to pound me faster and faster until I was screaming out in pleasure. The orgasm erupted inside of me, sending waves of pleasure through my veins. I gasped, digging my fingernails into his skin and feeling the hot juices inside me flowing down over his cock. He looked deeply into my eyes and grinned, tightening his hold on my ass and pulling away from the door.

He carried me across the room and laid me down on my back on the bed, pulling himself over me, his cock still deep inside. Slowly, he picked up each of my legs, one at a time, kissing my thighs and laying my ankle over his shoulder. He leaned forward and pushed in deep, grabbing onto my tits and squeezing them. I tilted my head back and moaned, never having felt anything as amazing as he did in that moment. Then, he opened his eyes and started to thrust again, this time with force and vigor. Our bodies slapped into each other over and over, echoing through the room. I reached out to both sides and grabbed the comforter tightly in my fists. I looked up at his hard body, his muscles flexing and releasing with every push. He was the hottest man I had ever seen, and it only made me want him more.

He unhooked my feet from his shoulders and bent my legs at the knees, pushing down on them and opening me up wide. I bit my lip and reached up, running my hands through his hair. He put his hands on both sides of my face and began to pump his hips up and down. I could have kept going like that all night long.

Chapter 19

I PRESSED MY BODY DOWN into Emilia's tight, pink pussy, feeling the warmth of her juices pulling me in farther. I had never felt something so amazing in my entire life, and though I wanted to take my time, I felt myself losing control. I fucked her hard against the bed, slowing down and pulling out. I leaned forward and kissed her lips, sucking on her lower one as I sat up. I reached down and rolled her over onto her stomach, pulling her ass up into the air. She looked back at me and bit her bottom lip, pulling a growl from my chest. I pushed my cock even deeper inside her, breathing heavily and listening to her deep moans. She reached between her legs and started to rub her clit, closing her eyes and wailing in pleasure. I didn't know how long I was going to be able to hold on. I grabbed her hips and pumped faster and faster, feeling her body convulsing beneath me in orgasm. She moaned loudly, her pussy contracting tightly against my shaft. I pumped harder, nearly reaching my peak.

As she moaned out louder, dropping her hand to the bed and shivering from her climax, I pushed in deep and held it there for a few moments before pulling all the way out and jacking my cock. She turned over quickly onto her back and smiled at me, watching my hot seed blow all over her tits and stomach. She rubbed her hand through it seductively, and I shuddered as the last bit dripped out of my cock. I reached up and leaned on her knee, catching my breath and chuckling. She smiled up at me with those beautiful eyes sparkling, and I jumped up to grab a towel and clean us both off.

I came back to the bed and pulled myself in behind her, wrapping my arms around her waist and holding her tightly against me. It felt so perfect, so right, and I never wanted to let go of her. Back in New York, I was a healthy young man, sleeping with my fair share of women. Never in my life, though, had I ever slept with someone like Emilia. She was gorgeous in ways I didn't know someone could be, and just the sound of her moans during sex made me want to come all over myself. She had bewitched me, and I didn't mind in the least. In fact, if she asked, I would beg her for more because whatever she was doing, it was reeling me right in.

I had just had sex with her, just gotten through the first of hopefully many times that I would be making love to this woman, but I still wanted more. My cock wasn't really in agreeance right at that moment, but I could see many all-night sexual encounters with her in the future. I honestly felt like I could make love to her for days, wrapped in those blankets, looking out over the vineyard and still want more. I felt like a teenager again with a libido off the charts, but I knew it wasn't me doing it. It was her.

When I had gotten my breath back, and my heart had slowed down, I rolled onto my back and she turned over, laying her head on my chest, her body close to mine. I pulled the covers up over us and ran my hand through her hair, smiling at her. There were no words between us, but I didn't think any words really needed to be said. Emilia fell asleep right there on my chest, breathing deeply with her leg intertwined in mine. I watched her sleep thinking about how beautiful she was until I, too, finally gave in and drifted off.

In the morning, the light shined through the windows and across my face, waking me from my sleep. I looked down. Emilia was still cuddled in my arms, her hair wild and all around her. She hadn't woken yet, but that was okay because I was more than happy to wake her up. I leaned forward and began to gently kiss her face, one small peck at a time. I moved over her forehead and down to her cheek, pressing my lips lightly against hers. She groaned, smiling but not opening her eyes. I moved over, kissing her lips and feeling her kiss me back. She lifted her hand up to my face and pressed her mouth firmly to mine, running her tongue across my lips. It was sensual and hot, and she rolled over on top of me, straddling my waist and kissing me wildly. I could feel my cock immediately get hard again, pushing against her back as she ran her tongue over mine, passion in her kiss.

I pulled my hands up her thighs and over her waist, pushing down on her. She moaned into my mouth, her body grinding against mine. I loved that she was so passionate, so erotic in nature. Everything she did was like a seduction, or at least that was how I saw it. She reached one hand up and pulled her hair back beginning to rock her hips against my skin. She breathed deeply into my mouth, and I rolled her over on her back, our lips still closely locked. I pulled back and looked into her eyes, smiling.

"Well, good morning to you too." I chuckled.

"Mmmm," she said, kissing me again. "Good morning."

"We have to get going on this getting ready thing, so why don't we roll this over into the shower?" I said.

"Sounds hot and steamy." She giggled, biting her bottom lip.

I growled, shook my head, and pulled myself from the bed. She watched me with a sexy smile as I disappeared into the bathroom. I turned on the shower and got in, feeling the hot water running over me. Just moments later, she got in behind me, running her hands down my chest and gripping my cock tightly. I groaned, feeling her hand sliding up and down it, wanting more and more. I turned and picked her up by the waist, setting her up so she was standing with her legs spread on both sides of the tub. I started to finger her, watching her throw her head back and growl. I watched, stroking my cock as she climbed further and further toward orgasm. Just as I thought I had her there, there was a knock on the door. She let out a deep exasperated groan, and I chuckled, jumping out and seeing who it was. I cracked the door slightly and poked my head out.

"Hi," I smiled at the innkeeper.

"Good morning," she said snobbishly. "I wanted to let you know that breakfast will be ready in ten minutes."

"Gotcha," I said, nodding my head and closing the door.

"She summons," Emilia said, standing in the bathroom doorway in a towel.

"That she does, milady," I said with a bow.

She smiled and pulled out some clothes, figuring we should get down there before the woman came back. Breakfast was delicious, and she made all the best stuff from pancakes to muffins. It was very much needed after the vigorousness of the night before. I didn't even realize how starved I was until I sat down at the table.

"Okay," Emilia said, eating some bacon. "What is the difference between a snowman and a snow woman?"

"I don't know." I chuckled. "What?"

"Snowballs," she said already laughing.

"That was good," I said, shaking my head. "Here's one. What do you call birds that stick together?"

"I don't know," she said, giggling.

I laughed. "Vel-crows."

"Ohh," she groaned and giggled at the same time.

We traded more jokes and laughed through breakfast. I was already disappointed that we had to leave so soon. I could have stayed there for a week and not gotten tired of it. In fact, with as beautiful as the place was and with as much as I loved it there, I could probably stay there for an eternity. Hell, I had enough money to do it, to retire and never want for anything. Maybe I should buy the place, and we could stay there together, ignoring the rest of the world and just enjoy the sunshine and the peaceful quiet of the place. I wasn't sure if she would go for that, but I sure felt like I was down for the idea.

I sat up in my chair and cleared my throat, shoving another piece of bacon in my mouth and chewing like crazy. My own thoughts had caught me off guard, and I didn't know where they had come from.

One of my main rules in life at that point was not to get tied down, not to find myself pinned into a situation with a woman. With Emilia, though, it wouldn't be her pinning me down and might possibly be the other way around. Which was something completely shocking to my psyche. My mind did not work that way at all, at least on a normal basis.

I had never, in my entire life, had thoughts like that, forever thoughts, about a woman. I knew one day that I would eventually settle down, maybe have some kids, but it hadn't ever really crossed my mind like it had just done. I figured when I finally did bite the bullet, it would be with some rich socialite, the kind who were constantly trying to tie me down, the kind who already knew how to live with wealth and would be happy with simply having a fat bank account and a successful husband. The kind of woman who ended up like the innkeeper, alone and bored in her late forties or early fifties and running a bed and breakfast just to see if she could do it. That wasn't Emilia, though, not in any way, shape, or form. Emilia was independent, didn't care about money, and had goals and dreams for the future beyond finding a husband and raising some kids. I couldn't believe how much this one woman had completely thrown me for a loop. Seriously, she had pulled the rug right out from under me, and I didn't even see it coming.

"You okay?" She giggled. "You went to another planet."

"Yeah." I laughed. "Sorry. I'm back."

"Good," she sighed. "We should probably go get packed."

"All right," I groaned. "If we must."

"We must," she sighed, standing up and reaching down for my hand.

We went back to the room and packed up our bags in silence, both of us feeling the sting of the reality of having to go back. When we were all packed, I carried the bags down to the SUV and loaded them into the back while Emilia signed out at the front desk. I leaned up against the car and watched as she walked out onto the porch, the sun hitting her perfect, pale skin. I shook my head, not believing how lucky I had gotten. She walked up, and I wrapped my arms around her, pulling her in close to me.

"Thank you for joining me for the night," I said. "I had an amazing time. Like, beyond amazing."

She smiled. "This place is pretty magical, isn't it?"

"You're pretty magical," I replied, unable to stop myself from leaning forward and giving her a deep, passionate kiss.

She melted into my arms as we stood there in the morning sun, getting ready to head back to reality. When I pulled away, she kept her eyes closed for a moment, a smile moving over her lips. She was really something else, and I had to fight myself to let her go. I did, though, and helped her in the car before jumping into the driver's seat. She reached down and grabbed my hand, smiling and nodding her head. I nodded back and pulled down the dusty dirt road, making our way back to Bonanza.

Chapter 20

Emilia

I SAT IN MY KITCHEN on Tuesday morning, staring down at my coffee. I looked up out the back window and put my chin on my hand, sighing deeply. I already missed Lucas, and he had just dropped me off the night before. He had some really crazy phone conferences in the morning, so he thought it better not to stay the night, and with Janson back in the picture, I had reluctantly agreed. Things were getting serious really fast between the two of us, and I couldn't seem to find the willpower to slow it down at all. It was too perfect in each moment. I found myself thinking about him pretty much during every minute of the day and night.

I had gone to bed the night before thinking about him and the weekend that we'd had. I dreamed about him during the night, waking up and wishing he was there beside me. In the morning, he was the first thing that popped into my head, and the butterflies in my chest got me moving with a little extra pep in my step. Still, having him on my mind was not nearly enough to satisfy me. I needed him to be close, to feel those big, strong arms wrapped around me. I had never felt so safe than I did when I was with Lucas, especially after he'd saved me more times than I could count at that point. He was like the white knight who stuck around because I was a bit of a damsel in distress.

When I had broken up with Janson, I'd put the idea and thought of a man in my life completely out of the picture. I focused on my future, on making the practice bigger and better, and of taking care of those horses at the stables. I wanted to not think about love or relationships or men at all, especially after I'd gone through what I had gone through with Janson. It didn't come to be a hard task, though. Before Janson, I had been asked out on a regular basis, but after him, not a single man came around looking for a date. I really hadn't even noticed until right then when I started to think about it. In fact, Lucas was the first guy who had pursued me since Janson. Part of my ego was a little bruised by that revelation, but at the same time, it didn't really make sense. It had to be connected.

Janson hadn't wanted to break up, but he was too stubborn and too cocky to ever say that to me. From what it looked like with Lucas in my life, it wouldn't surprise me at all to find out the sheriff had been scaring off any man who was in the least bit interested in getting to know me better. Now that I realized it, I was shocked anyone had bid on me at all during the auction, especially with Janson lurking around. Lucas had, though. He'd stood right up and saw the worry in my eyes, saw the awkwardness that ensued when the sheriff was bullying everyone out of bidding. He didn't take Janson's shit, and he didn't fold to the pressure of it all. He knew what he wanted, and no one was going to talk him out of it, not even the mega-asshole Sheriff Janson.

It was crazy how I felt when I thought about Lucas. It was like I already knew him, like I had known him all my life. It was the strangest feeling, especially since he had only been around a little over a week. I felt more comfortable around him than I ever had with Janson, and I knew everything about that man. There was one thing about Lucas, though, that I could tell from the first time I met him. He had a really good heart. He cared for people, and he wanted to protect people, protect me from the dangers of the world. He wanted to help people and make the world a better place. He was a billionaire, sure, but he was a man, a human being, first and that was really what drew me to him.

On top of that, his personality was to die for. I had never met someone over the age of ten who I could sit at the breakfast table with and crack corny and terrible jokes, but that was exactly what we had done at the vineyard. He was playful with me, not taking things too serious-ly, and his sense of humor was perfectly matched to mine. Most billionaires, not that I knew more than one, who happened to be Lucas, but most, I would assume would be pretentious, rude, and snobbish. Not Lucas. He was more down-to-earth than most of the people in that town. He never turned his nose up at anything, and he was happy with fancy dinners or barbecue with plastic tablecloths. He never made me feel like I wasn't enough or like what I had wasn't enough.

I picked up my coffee and took a big gulp, shaking my head and laughing at myself. I was sitting in my kitchen all alone, talking to myself about how amazing Lucas was. I definitely liked him way more than I ever thought would be possible. In the beginning, I'd assumed it would be a fling of sorts with him, something fun, not too heavy, but I had long since spiraled past that level. Either way, it was what it was, and if I didn't get back to reality, I was going to be late for work. I stood up and took my coffee cup to the sink to rinse it out. I went back upstairs and started puttering around my room, getting dressed, and putting my things together for work. As I turned toward the bed to pull the covers up, I heard my phone ring by the bed.

"Good morning, best friend," I said, seeing Alison's name on the screen.

"Oh. My. Shit," Alison said in a panic. "I cannot believe what is going on. Did you look at the news today? Do you know what this means? Emilia, holy shit, you need to say something. I am totally freaking out over here."

"What?" I said, shaking my head.

Alison was talking so fast that I could barely understand anything she was saying. She was in a complete tizzy over something, but what that was, I couldn't figure out for the life of me. She started all over again, going on a complete rampage, saying something about the news.

"Alison," I shouted to calm her down. "You have got to take a deep breath and slow down. I cannot understand you."

"Okay, okay," she said, breathing heavily. "I'm sorry. I'm just so excited. I could barely believe my eyes."

"What happened?"

"So, I woke up this morning and made my coffee and sat down to peruse the internet like I always do," she said. "I looked through Instagram, and it was boring as usual, and then Facebook, but that was boring too. I completely ignored the trending stuff on the right, which probably would have led me to the discovery much sooner."

"What discovery?" I said annoyed.

"Emilia, just go check out the news, Twitter, Facebook, whatever," she said. "You, my friend, are freaking famous."

"You've really lost it," I sighed, grabbing my laptop off the shelf and opening it up on my bed.

I signed into my Facebook and started slowly scrolling through, realizing my inbox was full of messages. I opened another tab and did the same with Twitter and with Google News. It turned out that the media was filled with stories about a billionaire bad boy's new girl toy. I was completely mortified as I pulled up one of the pictures and blinked at it. There must have been a photographer somewhere around the vineyard because splashed across every page was a photo of Lucas kissing me in front of the bed and breakfast. It was right before we were leaving, when he took me in his arms and kissed me passionately.

"I'll call you back," I said in a monotone voice before hanging up the phone and dropping it in my lap.

I sat there on the bed just staring at the picture, the colors, the way he was holding me tightly around my waist. For shit's sake, even my leg was bent, and my foot was in the air like some romance novel cover. It immediately brought back a very visceral reminder of that amazing kiss. I could almost feel his lips pressed to mine. I shuddered, bringing my hands to my mouth and gasping. It had been an amazing kiss, one that almost everyone in the world had probably seen by that point. One that showed my face perfectly, and there was no mistaking that it was me. Anyone who looked at it, anyone in the town would see it was me being kissed by Lucas.

I opened the story all the way and started reading it, trying to cringe at every savory word the author of the article had used to describe me. The story itself hinted that Lucas was a lady's man, one who found a girl at every port, one who had picked me as his next girl du jour. I was being painted as nothing more than the flavor of the week or month or, maybe worse, the flavor of the day. I slowly shut my laptop and sat there with one hand across my chest and one touching my lips. I felt shattered, broken, exposed, even from that story and that picture. I felt like everything I had thought to be true was nothing more than a love affair while he was off playing in Oregon. I felt completely and utterly shamed by the people who'd written the articles. They had no idea who I was or what Lucas and I had.

Not only did it make me look like a joke, it splattered my private life throughout the public eye. I had even had a conversation with Lucas about that, about how I could never deal with being pulled apart and judged by everyone out there. I saw the comments on social media. They were not kind, and they definitely weren't defending me in any way. If that was the way the media immediately portrayed Lucas's relationship with me, then maybe I was wrong about everything. They didn't report that he had a girlfriend or that he was seeing someone. They reported that I was just one in a steady, revolving door of women. Maybe things weren't all they were cracked up to be. Maybe what we had wasn't what I'd thought in the first place, and I really was just another girl in the line. Maybe, just maybe, I let love blind me to the point where I didn't know Lucas as well as I thought I did.

I shook my head and took a deep breath, figuring the best thing to do was to get to work and get my mind off things. But as I pulled into the parking lot of the practice, things went from bad to even worse. The sheriff's car was parked out from, and Janson was waiting for me outside. I got out of the car and tried to keep myself calm, but he cornered me, a look of anger on his face.

"What the hell are you doing with your life?" he said. "I wake up and find that my ex's face is splashed all over the tabloids like some common whore."

"I have to go," I said, pushing past him into the clinic.

I felt like total shit, like I had been completely humiliated. My day was terrible, and it had only just begun. I was starting to think I should have stayed in my bed.

Chapter 21

Lucas

"OVER HERE IS WHERE all the computers are being set up," I said, pointing to the right.

I was doing a group interview with a bunch of journalists and showing them around the facilities. It was only an hour after I had a ton of conference calls to take, so at first, I wasn't looking forward to it at all, but it wasn't actually going that badly. Everyone was attentive, listening to everything I said, snapping pictures of everything, and walking along quietly. Not a single one of them even so much as mentioned Natasha or any of her bullshit allegations. I figured that maybe it had finally blown over or maybe my PR rep had finally sent me a bunch of professionals to look over the facility. But, as always, there was another surprise waiting in the wings, one that I was not expecting in the least. I stopped and turned toward the group, about to take another round of questions from them. A young woman in the front raised her hand, and I nodded at her.

"This question is just a little off the topic of your company, but I know everyone wants to ask it," she said.

"If it's about the Russians, I've already said my piece," I said.

"No," she said with a smile. "Not about the Russians. We wanted to know about the identity of the woman you were photographed kissing in the vineyard not far from here."

"I'm sorry? What picture?" I said, looking down as the journalist showed me on her tablet. "Uh, I would really prefer not to comment on that. Next question?"

"The woman has been identified as a local veterinarian," another reporter shouted out, looking down at her notes. "An Emilia Willow.

She's apparently considered a pillar of the local community here in Baxter. Would you like to give a statement on your relationship with her? Are you dating?"

"Listen," I said, shaking my head. "I think that I have revealed enough about my life over the last six months with the Russian scandal. I want to ask that you and other journalists consider respecting my private life. Now, if there aren't more questions about the facility, I'll show you the way out."

I ignored the questions flying at me and nodded at the security guard standing close by. I turned right down the hall, but he stopped them from following, showing them back out the front doors. I headed down to my office and closed the door, sitting down behind the desk. I leaned back in my chair and closed my eyes, shaking my head. Just the mention of Emilia's name brought back all the thoughts and feelings that had not been far from the front of my mind since I'd dropped her off the night before. She never really left my mind, and apparently, now she was on the mind of a whole lot of people.

I turned in my chair and pulled up my Facebook account, scrolling through the picture of us kissing. Every major outlet had run the story, and they didn't make me or her look good in any kind of light. I slammed my fist down on the desk and leaned back again, looking up at the ceiling. I had really enjoyed my time with Emilia, maybe too much, in fact. I had found myself thinking about forever with her at the vineyard, kissing her like I planned on doing it for a lifetime. All the while, the real world was lurking right around the corner, popping up to remind me I wasn't the kind of guy who got the happily ever after, no matter how much money I had in my pocket.

Emilia was too wholesome, too good of a person to end up with someone like me. She had a heart of gold, the kind of woman who would give her last dollar to someone to help them out. She wasn't the kind of girl I was known to be with, and now everyone was going to see her in a completely different light. None of them were going to know how amazing she was and how I didn't deserve even a second glance from a woman like her. No one was going to give her the benefit of the doubt. I had been an asshole for my entire life, no matter what my intentions had started out to be. I had done things I was not proud of, especially back in my old neighborhood. I'd had to help my mom keep the lights on, and I'd had to do anything I could to help put food on the table and keep things flowing in that house. I grew up long before I was supposed to, and I learned how to live life and how not to live life, and all because of the situations I'd found myself in through the years.

Emilia had a future ahead of her, a life, a future family, a practice that she had built, and she did all of without ever treating anyone poorly. If I stuck around in her life, I would do nothing but drag her down, down, and down until everything she had worked so hard for was ruined. That was what I did, that was what the media did to unsuspecting people like her. They pushed and pulled until they had taken the last bit of a person, and when the story was done, they walked away, never looking back. No matter how hard my life had been, my mother had taught me better than that. Hell, just seeing how she wasn't treated fairly was enough to make me know better. Emilia deserved a good man, better than I could ever be. The least I could do was try to be a good person and call things off with her before she lost everything and everyone.

I owed her that, and so much more. I had come into her life, forced my way in, and now she was paying the price for the fact that I didn't think things through like I should have. How I didn't get a call from PR when this story first leaked was beyond me. At least then, I could have stopped it, slowed it down, or something. But no. I found out hours after it had been published. I sighed and put my head in my hands, shaking it back and forth. Almost as if the rep was psychic, my office phone rang, and it was her.

"I seriously want to know why no one caught this story when it first went out," I said angrily. "I just found out about it during a group interview with a bunch of young, idiot reporters."

"I tried to call you this morning," she said. "But you must have been out of range. Why in the world do you sound so angry?"

"This is just what I need, more bad press, and to top it all off, this girl is actually a really good person," I said.

"First of all, this is not bad press," she said. "It's playing out really well in the press. Secondly, if you find the real journalists who actually did their research, you would see they talked about her as an upstanding member of the community. A civilian to royalty kind of enchantment to the story. I like it, Lucas, so stop freaking out. I want you to keep it up."

"That's not possible," I said. "I'm leaving town really soon, so this relationship, it's not sustainable."

"So, bring her back to New York," she said.

"There's no way she would agree to that," I said. "Her life is here in this small town. She has a practice, she's happy here, and the last thing she wants is to be dragged to the city and made the center of attention."

"I need you to reconsider leaving then," she said. "Please, Lucas. You know I don't beg, but I'm begging you right now. We have killed ourselves trying to get an ounce of good press, and now that you have it, you want to run from it. You owe me this."

"No," I said. "I pay you to kill yourself for good press."

"Come on," she groaned. "Staying a couple more weeks in Bonanza is not going to kill you. A couple of weeks with this Emilia girl will do more to erase all the bullshit of your past faster than a thousand green energy projects will."

"Are you serious?"

"Heart-attack serious," she said.

"Fine, I will think about it," I said. "But you need to know this can't go on forever. I'll call you later."

"You're my hero," she said before I hung up the phone.

Holy crap, how did I go from being the villain, allegedly working with the Russians, to being America's sweetheart love story overnight? It was frustrating and unbelievable, and I knew Emilia was going to hate it, every second of the press. I didn't know what to do. I liked her, more than liked her, in fact, and beyond just hanging out and laughing with her, I loved the idea of another passionate night of sex with her. It was dangerous, though, and it could end in a bad way with a lot of hurt feelings. At the same time, I couldn't get this girl off my mind, and ever since we got back from the vineyard, I had been dreading the idea of leaving her and going back to my old life in the city. I hated to even think about not seeing her anymore and letting everything that we had become float away like it never happened.

I sat up in my chair and put my hand to my chin, thinking about what the PR agent said to me. Maybe all of this was a sign, and maybe she was the right woman to help me with this transition into a better, stronger life. She already made me want to be a better man, to help others like she did, to remember where I came from and to stay humble when the rich part of me tried to take over. I had never been that careful with anyone in my life. Maybe I needed Emilia to continue along that path, a woman who was sweet, honest, and accepting. Someone who didn't make me feel like shit because I had too much money or not enough money. The girl didn't give two shits about my bank account and could sit at a breakfast table laughing at corny jokes with me over pancakes and muffins.

I had never met anyone like her before, and I had a feeling I wouldn't again. She was a one of a kind person and the kind of woman who didn't exist in the world anymore. She was exactly what I needed, and I didn't even know it until she was right there in my arms. There was no real way I could walk away from her, no matter how hard I tried to tell myself I could. I had to be resolute, and I knew I wanted to take my relationship with Emilia to the next level, even if that meant being in Bonanza longer than I expected.

A warmth filled my chest thinking about having more time with her, showing her how much I cared. I needed to do something special for her, especially after what happened today. I thought about it for a second and then remembered our conversation at the barbecue restaurant. That was it. I would stop by her house that night with supplies and cook her a home-cooked meal.

Chapter 22

Emilia

I TRIED TO GET A HANDLE on everything after walking into the office that morning, but I just felt off all day. I was completely rattled by the news coverage showcasing my and Lucas's trip. Not to mention that Janson had cornered me that morning and pretty much called me a whore because I was photographed kissing another man at a vineyard. He was the last person I had wanted to see, which was my luck since he was the first one who had popped up that morning. So much for him not finding out about me and Lucas or our getaway to the bed and breakfast. There wasn't a person with internet access who wouldn't have heard about it by then.

Not only did I have to deal with my phone ringing off the hook and messages popping up all over my email and my social media accounts, my own vet office was abuzz with the news. Everyone who worked there knew me really well, and they knew there was no way I was going to talk about what happened. But still, I could hear them whispering in the back, and every time I walked up to the front counter, they would stop whispering and act like nothing was going on. I considered shutting them all down but decided the best course of action was probably to play it off and try to get through the rest of the day. It was difficult with even the customers whispering about it.

About halfway through the day I finished up with a surgery on a dog's broken leg and walked up to the front, ready to take a lunch break. I let the receptionist go for lunch and figured I would sit at the front and read through the afternoon client files. As I was sitting there, the front door opened, and a woman walked inside, looking around. When she saw me, she smiled nervously, picking up her chihuahua and setting him on the counter. I didn't recognize the woman, which was strange since I knew everyone in town. People from outside Bonanza didn't really come see me unless it was a livestock issue since there were vets in all the surrounding towns. I figured maybe it was a fluke, or maybe she was just visiting. We seemed to be having an influx of visitors from out of town lately.

"Hi," I said. "How can I help you?"

"My dog," she said, petting the pup. "He's been vomiting for a couple of days now. Not keeping down food or water. I figured I should bring him in and let the vet check him out."

"Okay," I smiled, standing up and looking briefly over the dog. "I'm sorry, you don't look familiar. Do you live in Bonanza?"

"No." She smiled. "I'm just visiting some relatives on the outskirts of town."

"Oh," I said. "Okay, where ya from?"

"Seattle," she said, shaking her head.

"I see," I said, lifting the pup's chin up and looking into his eyes. "Well, I'm the vet here, Dr. Baxter, and if you would just fill out a little bit of information for me, I can get your pup seen and hopefully taken care of pretty quickly. He seems to be in good spirits, so that's a good sign."

"Thank you," she said, filling out the paperwork at the desk.

When she was done, I put the info into the computer and then showed them back to the examination room. I put the puppy on the table and did my routine exam, checking for any signs of anything dire. It was strange, though. The dog didn't seem to be sick at all, and as I examined his teeth, I noticed he still had some food stuck in them. I stood up and put my hands on my hips.

"He's looking pretty well," I said. "I'll take his temp and rule out any viruses."

"Okay," she said. "Can I ask you something?"

"Sure," I replied looking down at the dog. "Do you know where Lucas Henry works?"

"Lucas?" I said, looking down at the dog. "He works at the ranch on the edge of town. Why? Do you know him?"

"No," she said, shaking her head.

I stood up and looked at her strangely, realizing I had most possibly been duped. The girl avoided eye contact with me at all costs. I looked back down at the pup and tried to play it off like I hadn't noticed.

"So, are you going to be working for the company?"

"No," she said.

"Then why are you looking for him?" I replied, looking up at her with raised eyebrows.

"Honestly?" She chuckled. "I'm a journalist. I came to town to get the scoop on what was happening between you and him. Would you mind making a statement or talking to me about your relationship to him? Is it serious?"

"I would mind," I said, going back to work on the dog. "My private life should stay just that, private, and I don't appreciate it being splashed all over the headlines without any warning. I'm not the girl they say I am, and that is off the record."

"I know it had to be a shock," she said. "To wake up to that, but if you would give me a few minutes of your time, let me ask you a few questions, then maybe you can clear up any misconceptions the press might have made about you."

"No thanks," I said taking off my gloves. "Is this dog even sick? Is it even yours?"

"Yes, it's my dog," she said, shaking her head. "But no, he isn't sick. I just needed an excuse to get in and see you. It's journalism. I didn't actually think you would welcome me with open arms."

"You're right," I said, slapping the gloves into the wastebasket.

"Just tell me one thing," she said before I could walk out of the room. "Tell me how you feel about all the scandals involving your new boyfriend."

"I have absolutely no idea what you're talking about," I said, turning around. "I know nothing about any scandals. And another thing, stop calling Lucas my boyfriend. He is not my boyfriend."

"You don't know about the scandal?" she said, looking at me like I lived under a rock. "It has been everywhere for the last few months. It's seriously been the biggest story in the media."

I felt like an idiot, and I didn't want to admit it to her, but no, I had no interest in reading about some rich guy and his scandals. I was a serious vet who owned her own practice and had more important things to do than read about someone else's life. I felt kind of like an idiot, though, seeing a guy who obviously had something huge in the past.

"I didn't hear about it, no," I said awkwardly. "Look, you have to leave. This is my business, and you're wasting my time. There are seriously sick animals waiting out there to be seen. You should be ashamed of yourself for bringing your pooch in here just to trick me into talking to you. So please, remove yourself before I call the sheriff and have him remove you himself. Trust me, I know the guy, and you do not want to have to deal with him."

She nodded her head abashedly, and I turned, walking from the office into the back. I couldn't believe how my life had been completely turned upside down over a damn kiss. Not even the kiss, a picture of a kiss. I had to end things with Lucas. I needed my life to go back to normal, so I could move on with my life. I nodded my head resolutely, feeling good about finally making a decision for my own good. As I sat there, though, staring at the laptop on my desk, I started to lose my self-control. This journalist was shocked I didn't know about whatever scandal Lucas was involved with. She couldn't believe her ears. That alone made me feel like a complete idiot, not to mention the fact that he had never once brought up anything about any kind of recent scandal.

Finally, after fighting myself for several minutes, I sighed and gave in. I turned the computer toward me and opened the browser. I typed Lucas's name into the search bar and held my breath as I pressed enter. The first things to pop up were all about me and the kiss, but as I scrolled farther down the page, I was more than surprised by what I had found. There were about a hundred different headlines talking about the Russians. I picked the most well-known publication on the list and clicked on it, reading through the story. My eyebrows immediately went up when I spotted the Natasha Noborov name printed on the screen. That was the name he had said when he'd told me about his ex-girlfriend. I kept reading, finding out that her father had been using Russian money to do all kinds of bad dealings. In the end, Natasha had not only accused Lucas of knowing about it but said he had been one of the investors with his father.

I held my breath finishing up the story, at least glad to see the government had cleared him of any wrongdoing. Still, it was way more in-depth than I ever imagined reading. I felt completely numb on the inside, like everything I knew about Lucas was a complete and total lie. How could I trust a man who couldn't even be honest with me during the privacy between us? I sat back in my chair and shook my head, not knowing what to think or say. I stared off into space, letting the numbness take over. My phone buzzed on the table next to me, pulling me back into reality. It was Lucas, and I wasn't sure if I should pick up or not. After about the third ring, though, I gave in and answered his call.

"Hey," he said. "Busy day at the office."

"Yeah," I said, still stunned. "Uh, what's up?"

"I thought I might stop by tonight if that's okay," he said.

I thought about it for a long second and then answered him. "Sure," I said.

"Okay, cool," he replied. "It's crazy here today, but I'll see you tonight."

"Okay," I said. "See you tonight."

I didn't want to see him, but I needed to confront him about everything. There was no way I was going to let him get away with this. The story he had told me the night he was trying to get me to open up about Janson was so far off what had actually happened that it might as well been a complete and total lie. In fact, he would have done better in the situation if he had told me a complete bullshit lie. At least then, I wouldn't feel betrayed like I couldn't believe anything that had come out of his mouth since I met him. I had been spending my time sleeping with, feeling safe with, a complete and total stranger.

I was going to confront him, let him know he was a complete asshole, and then I was going to end whatever was going on between us. I wasn't stupid. I knew he had played me, and boy, did he really get me good. He had me actually believing he was a stand-up guy, just trying to do good things. Whatever. It wasn't going to matter after that night. He would be gone from my life for good.

Chapter 23

Lucas

BEFORE I WENT TO EMILIA'S house, I stopped off at the general store and was able to pull together enough ingredients for a halfway decent dinner for the two of us. It was a really good thing I had spent most of my childhood throwing together nonmatching ingredients and making something that was halfway nutritious and not terrifying to eat. I knew she would appreciate it no matter how it turned out because she was the kind of girl who truly believed it was the thought that counted in situations like that. Still, I wished I had been able to figure out where the grocery store was, so I could really cook her something nice. I wanted to impress Emilia for some reason, and I knew money and flashy things wouldn't do it. She was down-to-earth and responded more to the little things, like cooking dinner, than any extravagant gift I could buy her. I really couldn't explain what about her made me want her to be impressed by me, but I had decided I was going to go with the flow on this one. Plus, I was just plain excited to see the girl and had been thinking about her all day, counting down the hours until I could meet her at her house.

I drove the SUV up in front of the house and got out, going to the passenger side and grabbing the bags out. I shut the door and smiled at my reflection, feeling the butterflies coming back. I turned and whistled, walking excitedly up to her door, making sure not squish any of the groceries in the bags. I rang the doorbell and looked around, happy to see no dead animals lurking in her driveway. When she opened the door, I turned, smiling widely.

"Hey," I said, my face dropping a bit when I realized there was definitely something wrong.

I ignored the look, figuring she could have had a really long day at work. When I had talked to her earlier, she sounded incredibly busy, and she was probably just tired. I bent down and kissed her on the cheek, feeling her immediately stiffen. I opened my eyes and pulled away slowly, feeling the reaction and taking notice. I wasn't used to seeing her like this, blank stare in her eyes, a cold demeanor toward me. Immediately, I went on high alert, expecting to hear about whatever it was very soon. Until then, though, I was going to act like I hadn't noticed a thing. She stepped to the side, and I walked into the house, smiling at her. I walked straight back into the kitchen and set the bags down on the counter and started to pull out the food and sort it into piles.

I could hear her walk into the room and stand there in front of me, but I tried not to meet her gaze. I had come to a revelation about her today, and I really didn't want anything to ruin it. I had a feeling, though, from the way she had her arms crossed in front of her, I wasn't getting out of it without a confrontation.

"What are you doing?" she asked coldly.

"I'm going to cook your dinner," I smiled cheerfully. "I don't know if you'll like everything, but if you trust me, I think you'll find I'm pretty talented."

I laughed to myself and looked up when I didn't hear a peep from her. She stood there staring at me, and for a moment, I really thought she was going to stop me. But, she turned, not saying a word and walking over to the kitchen table and sat down. I went through the kitchen pulling out the pots and pans. I got the water boiling, the pasta in there cooking, and started the meat sauce. The smell was amazing. Once that was rolling on its own, I wiped my hands and walked over to the table, pulling out the chair and sitting down in front of her. Emilia was just sitting there, looking down at her phone, not saying a word. I cleared my throat and sat back, waiting for her to initiate a conversation. When she didn't, though, I knew I was going to have to bite the bullet and ask her what was going on.

"Emilia," I said, reaching my hand out and touching her arm. "What's wrong?"

She looked over at my hand and then slowly raised her head, staring at me as if I had two heads. I retracted my hand very slowly and put it in my lap, sitting up straight in the chair. From the look on her face, I instantly knew it was way worse than I had originally thought. Whatever it was, it wasn't looking good for me either.

"Okay," I said. "It is obvious something I should know about, and I'm definitely not picking up on anything right this second. Can you give me a hint?"

She didn't say a word, didn't even crack a smile at my humor. She reached down to the table and pulled up the picture of us kissing and slid it across to me. I sighed and hung my head, figuring she would eventually bring it up.

"I saw it," I said. "I found out about it from a group of journalists I was interviewing with today. Honestly, I knew you might be a little upset, but I really didn't think that much of it. The articles by CNN and Newsweek and all the major publications talk about you in a very positive light."

I had been in the news plenty of times, so many, in fact, that I rarely even noticed when something came out about me. The only reason I had noticed that was because we had been on high alert ever since the Natasha thing. Sometimes, paparazzi followed me around. It was part of my life, and I had explained that to Emilia, not that it was her fault. I thought that all the way out in Central Oregon wouldn't be something that was worth the big-time reporters' time, but apparently, from the look of the picture, I had been definitely wrong.

"I'm sorry, Emilia," I said. "I'm sorry if you're uncomfortable with the photo. I would have never taken you there if I thought there was any chance the press would pick up on us being together. You have to know I would never put you in a situation like that on purpose, especially after you told me how you feel about your privacy. I've talked to my PR people. I made an express wish to the press in front of me to please let me have some privacy, and now I know that, apparently, there isn't any place too remote for them. We'll definitely try harder next time to avoid the press altogether."

She pulled the phone back across the table and looked down at the screen. I could tell she was thinking, and I really hoped it was for the better. She took a deep breath and looked back up at me.

"I don't think there will be a next time," she said coldly.

"What?" I said, sitting up. "You don't mean that. It was just one picture."

"Today, at work, I had a woman come in claiming her dog was sick," she said. "Turned out the woman was really a journalist trying to get close to me. She wanted to know about us, what we were to each other. I was angry, so I told her it was none of her business. But then she asked me how I felt about your latest scandal, and I was perplexed. So, after she was gone, I did some research of my own, and I figured out what she was talking about. What I found out shook me to the core, and I realized the little story you told me about your ex-girlfriend was total bullshit."

Immediately, my stomach dropped, and I felt my heart shudder in my chest. She had found the story about Natasha and the Russians. Not only had that story almost killed my company, it now looked like it was going to be my and Emilia's complete demise. I knew I had to at least try to explain. I couldn't just let it go.

"Look, I know those stories look bad, but when I told you about Natasha, I didn't want to get all crazy into the Russian oligarchy, the money, and all of that," I said. "Natasha only said those things because she was mad about the breakup."

"Don't you understand anything?" she said, shaking her head. "It's not about the scandal, and really it has nothing to do with the actual scandal. I know you aren't working with the Russians. It's about more than that. It's about who you are as a man. I'm upset about the way you treated Natasha and all the women who came before her. I'm a simple woman. I told you that from the very start. I'm a hometown girl who has a simple life and likes it that way. I'm not ready or interested in a sophisticated billionaire who uses women like they're toys and tosses them away when he gets bored."

"Emilia," I said feeling hurt by her words. "That's not at all what happened with Natasha, and that is definitely not what's happening be-tween the two of us. You have been there with me this whole time, and you've seen the bond and connection you and I have. You can't really believe I would do something like that to you, that I could fake those kinds of feelings and affections for a woman."

"Usually, in my life, I base everything on actions and not words," she said. "But when you lie to me about something important, some-thing that ultimately made me feel comfortable enough to open up to you about my own relationships, it definitely makes me not want to trust anything about you. No words, no emotions, no actions seem real to me at this point. How would I ever be able to look you in the eye and actually trust you again?"

"Emilia, please, I know it seems like that now, but I swear it wasn't," I said. "Give me a chance to prove it, to make all of this up to you."

"No," she said, shaking her head. "I don't want to live like that, and I don't want to live in the public eye like that. I already told you that from the beginning, that I wasn't cut out for a life in the media like oth-er women might be. That's just not me. Besides, you're going back to New York City soon, right? It's not like you're going to settle down in Bonanza, be a small-town billionaire or anything. We might as well give into the inevitable now and stop dragging this through the mud."

"I'm not ready," I said, shaking my head. "I don't want to end this. It's too important to me. You're too important."

"It was bound to happen anyway," she said. "We both knew that. We knew it from the beginning. I think you should just leave. I appre-ciate the dinner and everything, but I'm not hungry."

She stood up and walked over to the island, and I followed her, looking at the food bubbling on the stove. I wanted to rush over to her, pull her into my arms, and never let her go. I wanted her to see how much I cared about her, but as I took a step forward, she turned away and switched off the burners. I nodded my head, getting the hint. She wasn't going to reconsider this, and it was probably best that I leave. I reached over and grabbed my keys, stopping for a moment to look back at her and see her turn her face away from me. I hung my head and left the house, so disappointed that I could barely think. This was not at all how this ending was supposed to go.

THE END

Book 2 – Allure – Blurb

AFTER PLAYBOY BILLIONAIRE, Lucas Henry, finds himself falling for the small-town veterinarian, nothing seems to go right for him.

When Janson, Emilia's crazy ex with a sheriff badge becomes reckless and dangerous, Lucas decides Emilia needs to go somewhere safe.

Convincing her to leave is hard enough, but figuring out how to keep her there is a whole other story. Secrets begin to spill out to the press about Lucas's less than stellar past, and suddenly everything starts to unravel.

Can Lucas save his career, his livelihood, his company, and keep the girl? Or will the Big Apple take a bite right out of Emilia's hometown sensibilities?

Opposites Attract Series

Book 1 – Entrance
Book 2 – Allure
Book 3 - Enthrall

More by Roxie Odell:

BOOK 1 OF THE SINNER-Saint Series

On the way to work, Cheri Holt encounters two events she certainly didn't expect and isn't at all prepared for. First, she's robbed at gunpoint, and second, a good Samaritan by the name of Thomas Graham—the hottest man she's ever seen in her life—literally bursts out of the darkness and saves her from the bad guy.

Though her knight's armor is slightly tarnished Cheri is completely smitten, a damsel ready to undress.

Unfortunately, her impromptu bodyguard disappears, and so does the only witness who can back up her version of what happened during the robbery. The gunman is destined to walk free without any corroborating testimony, giving Cheri yet another reason to continue stalking her gorgeous mystery man. In a chance encounter and a passionate exchange, Cheri asks Thomas for his help, but this time the answer is no. He's a man with a past, which prevents him from being there to rescue her again.

He tells her to turn and walk away, but Cheri finds that an impossible thing to do. Their attraction is a once-in-a-lifetime kind of feeling, and they both know it. In the end, it's Thomas who can't let her go.

Just when it looks like they might be heading for a white picket fence future, his old ways revisit him, threatening to destroy the best thing that's ever happened to him...and to her.

Can Thomas and Cheri find the strength to love each other and share a future that might be tainted by the past?

BILLIONAIRE IN PARIS Series
BOOK 1 is FREE

It may seem impossible to have a bad day in Paris, but beautiful, smart Grace Delacourt somehow accomplishes that as she is reamed by her boss right there on the sidewalk of an outdoor café. When a handsome, charismatic man advises Grace to walk away from her job, she has no idea that the man, seemingly just out for a cup of coffee, is a billionaire shipping tycoon.

Tony Petrides, owner of Greek Tower in the Paris business district—a successful empire in its own right, with offices all around the world—whisks Grace away from her boss's screaming rant and turns her bad day into a memory that will stay with her forever. Unfortunately, their intense and unexpected romance is eventually derailed by a little white lie. Grace tells Tony goodbye, but when she returns home and finds herself unable to land another job, she is forced to accept a position on the West Coast, with Petrides Shipping, working one on one with the man himself.

Will their smoking-hot chemistry override past mistakes, or will one more lie finish them for good?

Weekend
of Romance

Weekend
of Passion

Weekend
of Kisses

Weekend
of Love

Find Roxie Odell:

NEWSLETTER:
http://eepurl.com/bHD6Vr
Facebook Page:
https://www.facebook.com/RoxieOdell

Don't miss out!

Visit the website below and you can sign up to receive emails whenever Roxie Odell publishes a new book. There's no charge and no obligation.

https://books2read.com/r/B-A-XEJC-BEMOB

BOOKS 2 READ

Connecting independent readers to independent writers.

Did you love *Entrance*? Then you should read *Unknown Identity Box Set: Books #1-3*[1] by Lexy Timms!

USA Today Bestselling author, Lexy Timms, brings you the first 3 bks of the Unknown Identity Series in a box set!

<u>Book 1 - Unknown</u>

Life has changed radically for Leslie. Her husband has finally succumbed to his terminal cancer and it's time for her to have a change of scenery. Moving across the country and setting up shop, Leslie takes the months to rebuild her life and figure out what she wants in the future.

Pouring herself into her successful mystery books series she's written, she is a reclusive global sensation writing under a penname.

Leslie realizes that her life is missing the romance she so desperately craved and now she's on the hunt to live her life beyond her grief.

Sooner than she realizes, cupid comes calling in the form of a handsome actor who has no clue she's a successful author. However, he comes with his own personal set of baggage.

Is new love possible after you've laid true love to rest?

<u>Book 2 - Unpublished</u>

Things with Conrad didn't go as Leslie has planned and after running back to New York City, she's the most surprised person in the world to find him standing on her doorstep, asking for a chance to win her heart over.

Leslie doesn't know how to respond. But, Conrad's here, alive and wanting to love her.

Excited to show her new found beau the city she's come to love, Leslie realizes when Amber and Josie return, that she left out one minor detail about her life.

The more Conrad expresses his love for her, the more Leslie grows nervous about telling him who she really is.

Will Conrad being willing to accept who she really is when the truth comes out?

<u>Book 3 - Unexposed</u>

All secrets have a price, and Leslie is about to find out when hers is exposed.

Now one of the most popular authors on the planet, Leslie only wanted to find life after love. She never expected that her heart would fall for anyone again.

Sexy, handsome, and an extremely famous actor, Conrad has managed to capture her attention, along with the attention of a million paparazzi who want to snap pictures of the couple together.

Can they survive the world known, published, and exposed for everyone to see?

SERIES:

Unknown

Unpublished

Unexposed

Unsure

Unwritten

Read more at www.lexytimms.com.

Also by Roxie Odell

Gambler Series Complete Box Set

Opposites Attract Series
Entrance

Player's Club Series
Billionaire's Baby
Billionaire's Baby Part #2
Billionaire's Baby Part #3
Billionaire's Baby - Player's Club Complete Box Set

Sinner-Saint Series
Strength
Sinner Saint Box Set

Watch for more at https://www.facebook.com/RoxieOdell/?ref=hl.

About the Author

Steamy Romance author Roxie Odell brings you heat, steam and romance in her stories. Be ready to sweat! Find her on Facebook: https://www.facebook.com/RoxieOdell/?ref=hl Follow her newsletter: http://eepurl.com/b9G7JX Twitter @roxieodellauthor

Read more at https://www.facebook.com/RoxieOdell/?ref=hl.